/If Andreas says even one thing/ can see that zit from/hope
it's pepperoni/ at four-thirty I have to/

A whirlpool of emotion ripped through Rae—
anger, anxiety, anticipation—and her heart fluttered
in her chest. She was a vegetarian. There's no way
she'd be hoping for pepperoni. And the Andreas
thing . . . Rae didn't even know anyone named
Andreas. Where were these bizarre thoughts—
thoughts and *feelings*—coming from?

She tried to stop the answer from coming, but it
slammed into her brain so hard, she could feel the
impact all the way through her body.

Was this how it had started for her mom? With
thoughts and feelings that didn't feel like her own?
Was Rae going to end up in a mental institution, too?
Was she going to die there the way her mother—

fingerprints™

gifted touch

melinda metz

AVON BOOKS
An Imprint of HarperCollins*Publishers*

Gifted Touch

Printed in the United States of America.

For information address
HarperCollins Children's Books, a division of
HarperCollins Publishers, 1350 Avenue of the Americas,
New York, NY 10019.

 Produced by 17th Street Productions,
an Alloy Online, Inc. company
33 West 17th Street, New York, NY 10011

Library of Congress Catalog Card Number: 00-193284
ISBN 0-06-447265-5

First Avon edition, 2001

AVON TRADEMARK REG. U.S. PAT. OFF.
AND IN OTHER COUNTRIES,
MARCA REGISTRADA, HECHO EN U.S.A.

Visit us on the World Wide Web!
www.harperteen.com

For Jane Cooper, who helped me become a writer

Rae Voight studied her palette, then dipped her brush into the deep purple paint, only dimly aware of the sound of the bell ringing and everyone else in her art class bolting for the door.

"I have to head over to the cafeteria. I'm on guard duty today," Ms. O'Banyon told Rae as she paused by Rae's easel. "But stay and work if you want. I love what you're doing here."

Rae didn't bother to glance up. She just gave her teacher a distracted grunt as the brush began flying across the canvas. Rae was in the zone, that place where it felt like electricity was running through her veins instead of blood. Nobody should expect her to talk right now. Nobody should expect her to do anything but paint. She jammed the brush onto the palette

1

again, really globbing on the oil paint, its pungent scent filling her nose. And then her hand was slashing the brush across the canvas. Faster. Faster.

Done. Rae let out a long, shuddering breath as she took a step back from the easel and studied her work. She'd been intending to paint the words in the style of an old-fashioned storybook—ornate capital letters, with maybe even some gold around the edges. But when she was in the zone, her hand had a will of its own, and the words had come off the brush in a psycho-killer scrawl. *Once upon a time, when we all lived in the forest and no one lived anywhere else . . .*

At least the writing matches the rest of the painting, she thought. When Ms. O'Banyon had assigned the class to do a landscape, Rae had planned to do a kind of fairy-tale forest, with beautiful flowers of improbable sizes.

The flowers were still there, but something was off about them, as if when they had grown so large and lush, they had also mutated in other ways, becoming sentient and greedy for even more size and power. One of the flowers had a dove trapped deep in the hollow of its dewy petals. Another's roots were wrapped around what appeared to be the slender leg of a fawn.

"Hey, Rae, do you really think it's a good idea to leave Marcus alone in the cafeteria?" a familiar voice called from the open door of the art room. "I mean, we're talking Marcus Salkow."

2

Rae quickly threw a sheet over her canvas and turned to face Lea Dessin. Lea was her best friend and everything, but Rae didn't especially want her to see the painting. Lea would just think it was weird, and weird was something Lea had a low tolerance for.

"I'd trust Marcus alone in the Playboy mansion," Rae bragged. She dunked her paint-smeared brush into a coffee can filled with water, then started unbuttoning the big white shirt she'd snagged from her dad—the one she always wore when she was painting.

"Oh, right. Now that you've grown breasts—unlike me—no guy can resist you. I forgot," Lea teased. Then, Lea being Lea, she strolled across the room and over to the easel, where she immediately reached for the sheet.

"There's nothing wrong with your breasts," Rae said, hoping to distract Lea, who had the capacity to discuss her breasts and other parts of herself—the frustrating straightness of her black hair, the unattractiveness of the line that ran from her waist to her hips—for multiple hours at a stretch. Which was pretty annoying sometimes, considering that for all Lea's complaints, she was gorgeous. Lean, with a face that was all angles—high cheekbones, pointy chin, perfectly straight nose—and amazing hair. She had that whole Lucy Liu thing going.

Lea didn't take the bait this time. She whipped off the sheet and studied the painting. Rae felt her stomach shrivel into the size of an aspirin. Paintings like this . . . They made Rae feel like there was another person living inside her. A person who was really and truly her mother's daughter.

Rae grabbed the sheet back from Lea and covered the canvas again. "Come on. I'm starving. Aren't you?" She steered Lea out of the art room, taking half a second to jam her painting shirt on one of the hooks by the door, then led the way down the hall.

"Check out what Kayla Carr has on," Lea said, her voice low. She jerked her chin at Kayla as she disappeared into the girls' bathroom, wearing an unfortunate trying-way-too-hard-to-be-cool retro seventies ensemble. "Maybe we should all chip in and buy her a lightbulb. Clearly she dresses in the dark."

"Clearly," Rae agreed, then felt a little spurt of guilt. *But come on,* Rae told herself. Kayla deserved it. It's not like it was hard to figure out what to wear. All you had to do was check out some mags and pay attention to what the non-socially-marginal girls had on. Rae was hardly Miss Live for Fashion. She'd be just as happy—happier, actually—in paint-stained sweats with her wildly curly auburn hair in a ponytail. But she was smart enough to know that that wouldn't cut it. In the critical summer between public school

4

sixth grade and private school seventh grade, she'd done the makeover thing. First the basics—the clothes, the hair, the makeup. Then the name—she'd started out the seventh grade as Rae, not Rachel, because Rae was more distinctive and because there was just something cool about a girl whose name sounds like a guy's.

She and Lea had become friends pretty much on day one of being Rae. Lea was a new girl that year. Rae liked that Lea didn't even have a flicker of memory of the somewhat dorky Rachel, the girl who'd drawn unicorns on the top of every single assignment she'd turned in. Unicorns with *names* printed under them—names like Flirtalina and Fabulousa.

"So tell me about last night," Lea said as they started past the mural that ran from the main office to the cafeteria. "You and Marcus disappeared from the party for quite some time, young lady." Lea nudged Rae with her elbow.

"Lea, there's this thing called privacy," Rae answered.

Lea flipped her chin-length, sleek black hair away from her face. "Just tell me one thing—did all your clothes remain on?"

"Yes. And that's all I'm saying," Rae answered. She veered toward her locker, which was across from the part of the mural that depicted all the wonderful

5

things Sanderson Prep graduates could do with their wonderful education.

Today Rae hardly saw all the ecstatic, super-achieving grads. Her mind was flooding with memories of last night with Marcus. There was this moment when Marcus had slid his hand under her shirt, and she'd felt like—

"Was there something you wanted to get out of there? Or did you just want to admire the form and line of your locker?" Lea asked, pulling Rae out of her thoughts.

A hot flush shot up the back of Rae's neck. *Get a grip*, she ordered herself. She reached for her lock, and her binder fell to the floor. When she bent down to snag the binder, her knees, which had become all quivery during her little mental visit with Marcus, didn't feel like they'd support her, so she pressed one hand against Amy Shapiro's locker for balance.

/Please, please, please, let me pass the physics test/

Rae jerked backward. Why on earth had she thought that? She didn't even take physics. But that little nerve in the corner of her eyelid started jumping the way it always did when she was panicked about a test she wasn't prepared for. Rae liked to be prepared.

"Are you okay?" Lea asked, a hint of impatience in her voice.

"Yeah. Fine." Rae grabbed the binder, shoved

herself to her feet, and dialed in her locker's combination. "I just want to grab that lipstick I borrowed from Jackie before French." She yanked open the locker door and grabbed the lipstick off the little shelf near the top.

/Rae thinks she's so special/

"What?" Rae demanded.

"What, what?" Lea asked, one of her perfectly plucked eyebrows arching up.

"Nothing. I just . . ." Rae let her words trail off. What was she going to say—*I just thought I heard someone saying something très snotty about me, then realized it was me thinking something très snotty about myself?* She slammed her locker shut and snapped the lock closed. "Never mind. Let's go." Rae strode toward the cafeteria. She used both hands to push her way through the heavy double doors.

*/If Andreas says even one thing/*can see that zit from/*hope it's pepperoni/*at four-thirty I have to/

A whirlpool of emotion ripped through her—anger, anxiety, anticipation—and Rae's heart fluttered in her chest. She was a vegetarian. There's no way she'd be hoping for pepperoni. And the Andreas thing . . . Rae didn't even know anyone named Andreas. Where were these bizarre thoughts—thoughts and *feelings*—coming from?

She tried to stop the answer from coming, but it

slammed into her brain so hard, she could feel the impact all the way through her body.

Was this how it had started for her mom? With thoughts and feelings that didn't feel like her own? Was Rae going to end up in a mental institution, too? Was she going to die there the way her mother—

"Are you waiting for a round of applause from the masses or what?" Lea asked, giving Rae a little push.

Rae realized she had frozen in place, with one hand pressed against her chest, as if that would slow down her heart. Trying to make it look casual, she dropped her arm back to her side. "Well, I did think everyone needed a chance to admire my new shoes," Rae answered, relieved when her voice came out sounding steady and . . . sane.

She stuck out her foot and turned her ankle back and forth, setting the beads on her denim clogs bouncing. Although with the tremors that were zipping up and down her legs, they'd probably have started bouncing, anyway. *See, you're fine,* she told herself. *If you're going crazy, you can't cover up that you're going crazy. So you're not going crazy.*

Rae led the way across the cafeteria to the frozen yogurt machine, grabbed one of the jumbo cups, positioned it under the French vanilla nozzle, and pulled down on the silver handle.

/It will be okay if I skip dinner and get on the treadmill the second/

A rush of dizziness left little dots of light exploding in front of her eyes. Rae squeezed her eyes shut. "Okay, stop it, just stop it. I've never even been on a treadmill."

"What?" Lea asked as she reached for one of the cheap plastic spoons.

Rae kept her eyes shut a second longer, then forced them open. She took in all the ordinary sights of the cafeteria, the tall windows overlooking the manicured lawns, the rah-rah banners made by the cheerleading squad, the same groups of people sitting at the same polished wooden tables, chewing, talking, laughing, harassing, studying, flirting—acting your basic normal. *Yep, everything is normal,* Rae told herself. *You're normal.*

"I didn't hear you," Lea said.

"I was . . . um, just talking to myself," Rae answered.

"You're losing it," Lea told her, carefully turning her cup in a circle as she pulled the handle on the yogurt machine, making a swirling mountain of fro-yo.

"You're right. I'm losing it," Rae agreed quickly, forcing her lips into a smile. She reminded herself that Lea wasn't trying to be sadistic. She didn't know about Rae's mom. Yeah, Lea was her best friend. But if Rae had told Lea the truth, Lea would be walking around with this armed nuke she could use against Rae whenever she wanted. Rae didn't plan to let anybody have that kind of ammunition against her. Ever.

Lea grabbed a handful of napkins and headed toward their usual table. Rae plucked a plastic spoon out of the metal container, then followed her, braced for the next moment of . . . She didn't allow herself to name the phenomenon she'd been experiencing.

But it, whatever it was, didn't come. As she followed Lea over to the usual table, all her brain murmurings felt . . . organic. Just regular Rae stuff.

Whatever the weirdness was, it's over, she told herself. She focused her gaze on Marcus. She always liked watching him when he didn't know she was looking. It made her want to grab a brush and try and capture the sprawl of his long legs, all the shades—from wheat to cream—of his close-cut blond hair, the perfect shape of his mouth, everything.

As if he could feel her staring at him, Marcus looked up, his green eyes locking on to her immediately. As soon as she was in reach, he snagged her by the waist and pulled her down on the bench next to him. Rae gave him a fast kiss. Their lips touched for only a second, but it brought back every sensation she'd felt lying on that bed at the party last night, giving her this sort of full-body blush.

"My parents have this cocktail thing after work, so the house is all ours tonight," Marcus murmured in her ear. His breath was hot against her earlobe as he waited for her response.

Except what should her response be? Rae wanted more of what she'd felt last night when they snuck away from the party. But more and the whole enchilada weren't the same thing.

"Actually my dad needs me home tonight," Rae lied. "Some kind of faculty get-together at our house, and he wants me to play hostess. You know, an end-of-the-spring-semester thing."

Marcus nodded, but his smile faded and he glanced away, turning his attention back to his lunch. Great—he was probably sitting there wondering how he'd gotten stuck with the immature girlfriend who couldn't just relax and—

"Hey, Do Rae Mi, did you remember to bring my lipstick?" Jackie asked from across the table.

"Got it right here." Rae dug around in her big straw bag until her fingers found the tube.

/Rae thinks she's so special/

The thought brought a bitter taste into her mouth. A bile and fro-yo blend. That was *not* her own thought about herself. This time she was sure. It had come from someplace else. But—

"Well, can I have it?" Jackie asked loudly.

11

"Huh? Oh, yeah. Sure." Rae realized she'd been in some kind of suspended animation, staring down at the lipstick in her fingers. She tossed the tube to Jackie, who caught it expertly, her light green nail polish glistening under the fluorescent lights.

Okay, so the—she couldn't stop herself from naming the phenomenon this time—so the insanity spell isn't over yet. *Just hang on,* Rae coached herself. *Ride it out.*

Rae forced herself to eat a little yogurt. That's what those who were not sanity challenged did at lunch. They ate.

"Could you pass me the salt?" Vince Deitz asked from the other side of Lea. He smiled at Rae, giving her a peek at his chipped front tooth.

"Not a problem," Rae answered. She could spoon yogurt into her mouth. She could pass the salt. No problem at all. She grabbed the yellow plastic shaker and—

/know I got a D on that Spanish quiz, maybe even an F/

—shoved it into Vince's hand. Her eyelid began to twitch again. She rubbed her eye fiercely. *Stop it! Just stop it! You don't even take Spanish, so you can't be freaking that you got a D.*

Her eye started to water, and she could feel her mascara beginning to streak. But the lid kept on twitching. And a tiny nerve on one side of her nose was twitching, too. And one in her lower lip.

12

No one can see, Rae told herself. *You can feel it, but they can't see it, so just hang on. Take a few more spoonfuls of the yogurt, then calmly stand up and go to the ladies' room. From there you can go home if you have to, but for now, just hang on.*

"Are you crying?" Jackie asked.

"Of course not," Rae snapped. She'd forgotten that her jumping nerves weren't her only problem. She probably had mascara down to her chin by now. "I just got something in my eye." Something like her own stupid fingers. Why had she rubbed so hard? Rae reached out and hauled the metal napkin holder toward her.

/My mother knows that I/

"My mother doesn't know anything!" Rae blurted out. "My mother's dead!"

The table went silent.

Rae's heart was pounding so hard, the sound filled her ears. The little twitches in her eyelid, nose, and lip began jerking in time to its thundering. "Sorry. Um, I just . . . Sorry." What else could she say? There was no sane explanation to give.

"That's okay," Lea reassured her. "No biggie."

Rae yanked a napkin free and started dabbing her weeping eye. But that didn't stop her from seeing that everyone at her table—the whole freaking crème de la crème—was still staring. And Lea, for all her "no biggie," looked faintly repulsed.

It's because she knows, Rae thought. *They all know. That's why they're staring at me. They can see it happening. They can see me becoming like her, like my mother.* Her breath started to come in short pants, as if her lungs were shrinking, as if her whole chest were shrinking.

Rae shoved herself to her feet. The napkin holder clattered to the floor. Automatically she climbed over the bench, bent down, and picked it up.

/My mother's going to kill me if/

"Why do you keep talking about my mother? Weren't you listening?" Rae shrieked. Now everyone in the cafeteria was staring. Whispering. They were saying she was just like her mother. Rae knew it.

A nerve in the back of her hand began to twitch in time with the others. Rae gave a howl of frustration and hurled the napkin holder away from her. It bounced twice on the linoleum floor. No one glanced at it. They kept staring at her. Because they knew the truth.

Marcus sprang up and started toward her. "No!" Rae screamed. "Stay back. All of you, just stay back. I don't know what I'll do if you come closer." She tried to pull in a breath, but her ribs felt like they'd wrapped her lungs in a tight, tiny cage. And her heart—how could it beat so hard without exploding?

"Rae, it's just me. It's Marcus," he said. He took one hesitant step closer.

"Get back!" Rae screeched. She saw Ms. O'Banyon running toward her. "You, too! Everybody just get back. I don't want to hurt anyone."

The way her mother had.

Marcus obediently backed up. Ms. O'Banyon stopped where she was, one hand reached out toward Rae. Everyone else just stared. Because they could see it. They could see the truth

They knew Rae had gone insane.

Chapter 1

"**I**s there anything you need for school tomorrow?" Rae's father asked as they drove down the freeway at precisely fifty-five miles an hour. "We could swing by the mall after your, uh, meeting. I'd be willing to give you control of my AmEx for, say, twelve or thirteen minutes." He took his eyes off the road long enough to give her something that she knew was supposed to be a smile, although it came out more like a grimace. Just way too many teeth showing.

That was your cue, Rae, she told herself. Her cue to launch into a long and elaborate whine-protest that would convince him just how key the right clothes and accessories were to having the kind of school year she'd want to look back on fondly when she was his age.

"What do you say?" her father asked. He rubbed the little mole on his right cheek, the way he always did when he got stressed.

"I'm good," Rae answered. She was sure there were some things she *should* want for the start of her junior year. A shirt in one of the "new" colors or a backpack upgrade or something. But she had no idea what the things she should want were. It seemed safer to stick to the stuff she already had. She could trust that Rae, the pre-freak-out Rae. But the only-days-out-of-the-hospital Rae—that was not someone who could be trusted with something as delicate as picking out appropriate clothes.

Her father's smile-grimace faded. "Well, if you change your mind . . ." He let his words trail off and studied the freeway stretching out in front of them with unnecessary intensity. Rae stared through the windshield, too, letting the waves of heat rising off the asphalt and the white lines flying past mesmerize her. Her happiest times, happiest post-freak-out, were moments like this—when she could blank out, her mind quiet. Which was pretty pathetic. She could just imagine her first day of school.

Hey, Rae, what did you do this summer?

Oh, I had a nice, long rest in a kind of . . . resort. And I took a lot of baths, which was fab because in the tub, my mind actually seems to work fairly non-psycho-ly. What about you?

And that was if anybody was even willing to talk to her at all after her meltdown in the cafeteria last spring. She'd seen Marcus only once since that day— hospitals gave him the creeps—although she'd gotten a couple of sweet cards from him. Lea had actually shown up at the hospital a couple of times—with a few other friends in tow—but she'd been better about sending an endless stream of little gifts. Not that Rae could blame her. A day at the hospital wasn't exactly the definition of summer fun.

"Could you hand me my sunglasses?" Rae's dad asked.

"Sure. You should always wear them when it's this bright. We blue-eyed types are so sun sensitive," Rae answered, doing her look-how-normal-I-am routine. She opened the glove box.

/What am I supposed to say to her?/

The thought was followed by a vicious wrench in the muscles between Rae's shoulder blades. A tiny gasp of pain escaped her lips.

"Are you all right?" her father demanded, his voice filled with needles of anxiety.

"Yeah, fine. Just banged my elbow on the door handle," Rae answered quickly. She'd managed to convince her dad and her doctor that the strange thoughts that had started slamming into her brain without warning were gone. And she wasn't going to give either of them any reason to suspect that she'd been lying; otherwise she'd be on the express train back to squirrel city.

"Sunglasses?" her father reminded her, sounding a little more normal. Neither of them sounded completely normal anymore.

"Oh, right." Rae snatched up her dad's dorky, geek-professor-attempting-coolness mirrored shades—

/a bald spot/

—and handed them to him, absentmindedly stroking the top of her head. She didn't try to figure out where the thought about a bald spot had come from. She'd given up on searching for explanations months ago and accepted the fact that this was her life now. All she could do was deal—and try not to foam unattractively at the mouth.

Rae focused her attention back on the heat waves and the white lines. But just as she was starting to reenter the blank zone, her dad changed lanes and moved onto the off-ramp. Three turns later the sign for the Oakvale Institute came into view. It was more low security than the hospital. No fences or anything. But Rae still bet it had that smell, that bargain-brand-disinfectant smell.

"I don't know why I even have to do this. I'm fine. Dr. Warriner said I was fine," Rae said.

"And you *are* fine," her father answered, his voice a little too loud. "You're doing great. The group sessions are just to help you keep on track, especially with starting back to school tomorrow." He pulled into the institute's parking lot and maneuvered the old Chevette into a spot almost in front of the main doors. "I'll be right here when you're done," he said, giving her arm an awkward pat.

Rae noticed he'd been touching her more since she got out of the hospital. She wondered if that was something Dr. Warriner had encouraged him to do in one of their private sessions. Rae wished her dad wouldn't bother. They'd never been touchy with each other, and now it just felt weird.

"See you in a bit," Rae answered. She climbed out of the car—

What's the point?!

—and started to shut the door. Her father reached over and held it open.

"I was thinking . . . or wondering . . ." His blue eyes looked hopefully up at her. "Maybe afterward we could stop off at The Wiz and pick ourselves out a television." He sounded like he was offering a five-year-old an ice-cream cone after a trip to the doctor for a booster shot.

But this was big. Her father was hugely, ferociously, adamantly anti-TV. Rae'd been begging for a set—just a little one for her room—for years. And now . . . Rae felt a lump form in her throat.

"TV is the opiate of the masses," Rae said, quoting him. "There will be no TV in my house." She turned and headed for the main doors before he could answer. Six months ago she'd have been ecstatic over the chance to be completely and fully TV literate and to get her daily dose of impossibly cute boys. But now . . . It would just be another sign of how much things had changed.

She hesitated when she reached the doors. *Got to do it,* she told herself. *Going to group will show that you're committed to your mental health.* Rae snorted. Maybe *committed* wasn't exactly the word to use. She shoved open the doors—

/*What a crock*/**sweater too tight**/ *Charmed on tonight*/

—and stepped inside, letting the hum in her head die out. Sometimes her bizarro thoughts came with this staticky hum. It was like having an electronic beehive in the brain or something. Other times the bizarro thoughts were loud and clear—no bees. Rae wasn't sure which was worse.

The middle-aged woman behind the reception desk smiled. Rae smiled back since that was what normal people did, and she wanted to look ultranormal. "I'm here for Ms. Abramson's group," she said.

"Down the hall, take the first left, then second room on the right," the woman answered.

Rae nodded, then checked the clock over the

woman's head. She had ten minutes, and she did *not* want to spend them sitting around with the losers. She spotted a bathroom as she started down the hall. *That'll do,* she thought. She stepped inside just as a girl with extremely short brown hair stepped out. Fashion choice? Or a grown-out hack job? Rae wondered. A couple of girls at the hospital had taken scissors to their heads.

She wandered over to the closest sink and stared into the mirror over it. This place was definitely lower security than the hospital. No way would they have allowed a patient in the same room with anything as potentially dangerous as a mirror, which could be broken to create knife-sharp blades.

"Looking good. Looking normal," she told herself. "Except for the talking-to-yourself thing." She washed her hands and dried them carefully with one of the rough brown paper towels, just to kill time.

No point in stalling anymore. If you're late, you'll probably have to talk for hours about what you think it meant that you were late. Could you have been experiencing some internal resistance? And blah, blah, blah.

Rae strolled over to the bathroom door and opened it.

/hate this place/

She snorted at the staticky thought. It wasn't hers. But it might as well have been. This was definitely a place that was easy to hate. And it did have that cheap disinfectant smell. She headed down the hall, trying to ignore the way her stomach was folding itself into some kind of origami creature. Way too quickly she reached the door of the room where her group therapy was going to be held. She walked through the open door without hesitation, head up, making eye contact with anyone she noticed looking at her, smiling back at the losers who bothered to smile.

Possibly I shouldn't call them losers, considering, Rae thought. *Maybe they're just like me, coming here because somebody said they had to, trying to get back to some semblance of regular life.*

She sat down in the closest empty chair—gray metal folding, of course—in the ragged circle, shooting a glance at the guy next to her. *Now, I'm sorry, but he* is *a loser,* she thought. *A Backstreet Boys T-shirt, and he has to be, like, sixteen or seventeen. Please.*

"Looks like the gang's all here," a thirtyish woman with black hair in dozens of tiny braids said as she strode into the room and shut the door behind her. "Except Jesse Beven. Know where he is?" she asked the Backstreet Boys fan.

The guy, helpfully, shrugged.

The woman shook her head as she turned to Rae. "I'm Ms. Abramson. And you're Rachel Voight."

"Rae," she corrected automatically.

"Okay, Rae," Ms. Abramson answered. "You'll get a chance to meet everyone in a little while when we go around the circle. But I want to start with an exercise."

There were a few muffled groans. Ms. Abramson ignored them. She turned her attention to the door, which was opening very slowly. "Glad you could make it," she said as a gawky redheaded kid who looked about thirteen sidled through the door, clearly hoping not to be noticed. Rae assumed he was the missing Jesse. He muttered an apology in Ms. Abramson's direction and took the seat on the other side of the Backstreet Boys guy.

"I want you to pair up," Ms. Abramson said as she headed toward the other side of the room. "And not the usual pairs, please. Anthony, you and Rae work together. Jesse, you team up with Matt. Nobody with anybody you've paired up with in the last three sessions. Are you listening, David and Cynda?" she asked a guy and girl across the circle from Rae. The two practically had *we're-a-couple* tattooed across their foreheads.

Ms. Abramson paused by the cupboards under the row of windows that lined one side of the room. She opened the center cupboard and pulled out a bunch of drawing pads and some boxes of crayons, then began handing them out to everyone in the circle to more groans, not so muffled this time.

Backstreet Boy—Anthony, Rae supposed she should start calling him—reluctantly hauled his chair around to face her. She scooted hers toward him, then shoved it back a little so their knees wouldn't touch.

"What I want you to do is draw a family portrait," Ms. Abramson continued. She reached Rae and Anthony, handed them supplies, and kept working her way from pair to pair. "And then draw a significant object in each person's hand—something important to that person. And no, Rebecca, I won't give you an example," she said to the hack-head girl Rae'd seen earlier. "There are no rights or wrongs. Just go with your gut instinct."

Cake assignment, Rae thought. She selected a couple of crayons—

/LIKE BLUE/*blister driving me nuts***/call Dan/**

—ignoring the flicker of random thoughts and the buzz underneath them, then handed the box to Anthony. He clearly had no interest in talking to her, which was a bonus. Rae decided to do her father first. High forehead. Nose with a bump. Bad posture. Thinning blond hair. She'd drawn him lots of times, and the sketch came out fast and easy. Choosing his significant object was a no-brainer—a book for the English prof.

Now me, she thought. That was harder. She wasn't

into self-portraits. *You're not doing this for Ms. O'Banyon,* she reminded herself. *Just get something down on paper, be the good little group therapy girl so you'll be able to stop coming sometime this century.*

Rae started to draw. Curly, reddish brown hair—lots and lots of it. Nose with a bump, like her dad's. Stubby eyelashes. Blue eyes.

Anthony reached over and took the brown crayon out of her fingers without asking. Rae ignored him, switched to another crayon, and kept drawing, so caught up, she hardly registered the alien thoughts. Mouth like Angelina Jolie's. *Like Mom*—the unwelcome thought flashed through her brain uninvited. Basic bod. And she was done. Now all she needed was her significant object, which was as much of a no-brainer as her dad's—a paintbrush.

"Can I get that brown crayon back, please?" she asked Anthony. "Just when you're done. Take your time," she said with pointed politeness. He immediately thrust the crayon at her.

/AM I LIKE HIM?/

A wave of yearning swept through Rae, and she felt the sting of tears in her eyes. She blinked rapidly. No way was she going to have a crying jag in her first day in group. *It's just one of your brain hiccups,* she told herself. *No biggie. Nothing to freak about. That feeling has nothing to do with you.* She forced herself

27

to return to her drawing. The handle of the paintbrush came out too long. It ended up as a root wrapped around Rae's ankle in the sketch.

"Just two or three more minutes, gang," Ms. Abramson called.

Damn. She didn't have time to start over. "Can I have the red?" she asked Anthony, then grabbed it without waiting for an answer.

/NICE HAIR/

Somehow that thought felt a little like the am-I-like-him thought. They felt like they could almost be from the same person. *They're not from anyone,* she reminded herself. The thoughts were in her own head.

Group therapy is no place to dissect your insanity, Rae told herself. *Your goal here is to put on the* Look How Normal Rae Is *show. So draw already.*

Rae drew a big red flower in the hand of the sketch Rae so the root would be coming from somewhere.

"Okay, time's up," Ms. Abramson announced. "Now, I want you to really study your drawings while you show them to your partner. Who are you standing next to? How close are you? Is one person in the drawing much smaller or larger than the others? What about the significant objects—what do they say about each person?" She gave two sharp claps. "So, talk among yourselves. Partners, don't be afraid to ask questions and make observations. But as always, no personal attacks."

Oh, great, Rae thought. *Why don't I just install a zipper from my throat to my belly button?* She shot an annoyed glance at Anthony. "You first, Backstreet Boy."

A dark flush crept up Anthony's throat, but he obediently held up his drawing. "This is me. And this is my mommy. And this is my daddy," he began in a singsong voice, pointing to one stick figure after the other as he spoke. "This is my half brother Danny. This is my half brother Carl. This is my half sister, Anna. This is my stepbrother, Zack. This is my stepfather, Tom. This is my previous stepfather, Rob. There are a bunch of significant boyfriends who were briefly family, or at least who lived with us, but I ran out of room."

"That's . . . a lot of people," Rae said.

"I'm so glad Abramson made us partners," Anthony answered with mock enthusiasm. He shoved his hand through his sandy brown hair and shot a glance over his shoulder, probably to make sure that said Abramson wasn't in earshot. "I can see that with your help, I'm really going to learn a lot about myself. When I leave here, I'll probably cry a little and then go do some work in a soup kitchen because I'll have realized there are worse-off people than me. And it will all be thanks to you."

"What's your problem?" Rae demanded. "All I did was make a simple observation—That's. A. Lot. Of. People." A loser with attitude. Could there be a worse combination?

"Your turn," Anthony told her, his dark brown eyes expressionless.

Rae shook her head. "Uh-uh. Not so fast. I get to ask questions." She studied his drawing. Make that his sticks with big circle heads. They all looked almost alike. But she was asking something. No way was she letting him off the hook. She jabbed her finger at the tallest stick figure. "This one is about twice as tall as the other ones. Which one is that again?"

"My dad," Anthony answered.

"Is he actually that tall?" Rae asked. "I mean, I know he's not a mutant who's double the size of other people. But is he a lot taller than average?"

Anthony jerked his chin toward Rae's drawing. "Why is that flower so huge?" he countered. He pointed at the red blossom. "It's bigger than the girl's head."

Rae automatically glanced at the flower and wished she hadn't. It was like the ones she'd painted in her landscape for art class that time—somehow more predator than plant.

"When it's your turn, you can ask what you want," Rae told him, forcing her eyes back to Anthony's drawing. "Now, talk. Dad. How tall?"

Anthony didn't answer. The muscles in his jaw were all tight, like he was grinding his teeth.

"So I'm guessing height is a sensitive subject," Rae said. "Does it make you feel inadequate that Dad is tall while you're . . . not?" Because Anthony was definitely short, probably shorter than most guys in his class. He made up for it in muscle, though. Rae couldn't help noticing that.

"Rae, Anthony, how are we doing over here?" Ms. Abramson called before he could answer. She came over and put one hand on Rae's shoulder and one on Anthony's.

Anthony tightened his grip on his drawing until the edges got crumpled. Rae considered repeating her significance-of-the-size question in front of Ms. Abramson. That would force Anthony to cough up some kind of answer, possibly winning some good-observation-Rae brownie points for herself. But her eyes were drawn to Anthony's clenched fingers, the knuckles white with strain, and she decided to give the guy a break.

"It's going good," Rae answered. "Anthony was just telling me that there were more people— boyfriends of his mom—that he should have drawn."

Ms. Abramson nodded. "Good sharing, Anthony." She gave Rae's shoulder a squeeze, then wandered off.

Anthony loosened his grip on his drawing, and it fluttered to the floor. Rae picked it up—

/AM I LIKE HIM?/

—and handed it over. The reception on that thought was good, she thought absently. Sometimes the thoughts were blurry, barely even clear words. Sometimes they were practically static—like the noise that came through on an out-of-reach radio station. But this one came through distinctly.

"So, which of these guys do you think you might be like?" she blurted out.

Wait—what had she just done? Am-I-like-him was a head thing, not an out-loud thing. *You can't do that, Rae,* she lectured herself. *If you do, if anyone figures out you're still having your brain seizures, it's welcome back to the funny farm.*

Where the hell had she come up with that question? Anthony shot a glance at Rae. It's what he'd been thinking about his dad when he drew the picture. He'd never met the guy—well, not that he remembered, at least. He'd been less than a year old when his dad bolted. But he'd always wondered if they had stuff in common. Which might be cool since he definitely didn't want to be like anybody else in his family.

"I'm not like any of them," Anthony mumbled.

He wished they weren't sitting so close together. Every breath he pulled in smelled like oranges. No, grapefruit. Who wore grapefruit perfume? It made the back of his throat itch.

"What about your dad?" Rae leaned forward and studied the drawing. "Don't you ever wonder if you're like him? I mean, I'm always wondering if I'm like my mom." Rae suddenly grabbed a crayon and began adding more petals to her freaky flower.

"He was a sperm donor. That's it," Anthony answered. He definitely wasn't going to spill his guts about how much he wished he could meet his friggin' daddy and then go live with him and—Anthony didn't allow himself to finish the thought. Way too pathetic. Besides, Rae wasn't even listening. She'd asked him a question, then started coloring away without even bothering to pretend she wanted to hear the answer.

"Okay. Flower. What's the deal?" he asked. He reached over and snatched the crayon out of her hand so she'd have to pay attention.

"I don't believe that you think of him as just a sperm donor," Rae said, finally meeting his gaze with her blue eyes.

"Good for you. Now I'm asking the questions," Anthony told her. "That flower is not normal. It's like out of a sci-fi movie. And is it attacking her—I mean you—or what?"

"It's just a flower," Rae answered. She folded her drawing in half so he couldn't see it.

"Bull," Anthony shot back.

Rae leaned closer to Anthony, getting right in his face. The grapefruit scent filled his lungs, grapefruit mixed with shampoo, and kind of a warm-skin smell. "And sperm donor isn't bull?" she challenged.

He didn't answer. She didn't say another word. And neither of them blinked. *Fine,* he thought. *She wants to have a stare down. Fine.*

Before either of them won the battle of the eyeballs, Abramson gave a couple of claps. "Good work, everyone," she called from the center of the circle. "I want all of you to bring your drawings home. Take a little time before next group to study them. You may be surprised about what insights occur to you."

Rae jerked her chair back around so it was facing Abramson. Anthony hauled his around, too, the metal chair legs squealing on the floor, then he folded up his drawing and jammed it into one of the front pockets of his jeans.

"It's time to go around the circle and hear how everyone's doing," Abramson announced. "Let's start with David today."

Anthony obediently looked across the circle at David, but his thoughts kept circling around to his dad, thanks to Rae and her stupid questions.

A couple of years ago he'd actually tried to find his father. At least he'd asked his mom some stuff. She'd started getting all teary, so he'd backed off and tried doing some Internet searches instead. But he didn't have enough info to track the sperm donor down.

"Anthony, do you have some feedback for Julia?" Ms. Abramson asked, snapping him out of his thoughts.

Man, she always knew when he wasn't paying attention. It was like she had radar or something.

"I think Julia needs to treat herself as well as she treats other people," Anthony answered, parroting what Abramson said to Julia practically every other session.

"I agree," Ms. Abramson said.

Anthony suppressed a smile. *Got away with it. Yeah.*

"Your turn, Rae," Ms. Abramson went on. "Just tell us how your life is going, what's coming up for you, anything you feel like sharing."

Anthony turned toward Rae. She sat up a little straighter and folded her hands in her lap. He couldn't help snorting at the good-little-girl pose, which earned him a head shake from Abramson.

"Well, I've only been out of the hospital a few days," Rae said. "I start back to school tomorrow. I'm

looking forward to it. I mean, I love Sanderson Prep.
I think it will really help me to get back in my old routine and see my friends and everything."

What bull. Anthony managed not to snort again.

"Any other feelings about going back?" Ms.
Abramson asked.

She knows it's bull, too, Anthony thought.

Rae used both hands to push her curly hair away
from her face. She raised her eyes to the ceiling, as if
she were looking for an answer graffitied up there.
"I'm a little nervous, I guess," she said finally. "But I
know I'm ready."

Total bull. Anthony waited for Abramson to call
her on it. But she didn't.

"We'll all be eager to hear how your first couple
of days went at our next session," Ms. Abramson said.
"That's it for today. I'm sorry we didn't get around the
whole circle. We'll make sure we get to everybody we
missed next time. And if anybody needs me, feel free
to call." She handed Rae a card. "That has my home
number on it and the number here. It's never too early
or too late."

Anthony didn't even get the chance to stand up
before Jesse was in front of him. "Got a new skate-
board. Want to see it? It's at reception. They wouldn't
let me bring it in."

I have three little brothers. I really don't need another

one, Anthony thought. But Jesse was basically cool.

"Sure," he said. "I've just got to take a leak. I'll meet you up there." He grabbed his jean jacket and headed for the door. When he stepped into the hall, he saw Rae up ahead of him.

"Hey, new meat," he called out, without exactly deciding to do it first. "Rae or whatever."

She turned around but didn't take a step toward him. *Trying to do her a favor and she has to be all snotty,* he thought as he headed up to her. But she had been decent when Abramson came up to them during that drawing exercise, so he kind of owed her one.

"If you want to be able to stop coming to our little parties anytime soon, you're going to have to start giving it up in group," he told her.

"What are you talking about?" she asked.

"I'm talking about how you're looking forward to going back to school and seeing all your friends. I'm talking about bull. Didn't you see Abramson's face? She wasn't buying it," Anthony answered.

Rae pulled the straps of her purse higher on her shoulder. She opened her lips, like she was about to say something, then snapped them closed.

"If you want out, you're going to have to put on the show. Talk about your *feelings.* Crying a little wouldn't hurt."

Rae didn't say thanks. Didn't say anything. Okay,

payback was over. If she didn't want to listen, forget it. He swung his backpack over one shoulder and started past her.

"It wasn't bull," she called out.

Anthony turned around to face her. "Oh, come on. We're talking school. You've got to know everyone's going to be talking about you on the first day back, staring at you, wondering if you're going to go nuts again. Somebody'll probably ask if they gave you electric shock."

The muscles in Rae's throat started to work. *She knows it's true,* Anthony thought. *She knows she was feeding us a line in group.*

"That's not how it's going to be," Rae insisted, but her voice came out husky, and Anthony thought he saw a sheen of tears in her blue eyes.

Great, Anthony thought. *This is what I get for trying to help somebody out. In another minute she's going to be blubbering, and I'll have to deal with it.* He twisted his head to the side, trying to crack his neck. "Look, I'm not exactly jumping for joy at the thought of going back to school myself. In fact, knowing I'm going to have to be there tomorrow makes me want to puke. It'll suck for you. But you'll live."

Rae's chin came up. "I really don't need advice from a guy in a Backstreet Boys T-shirt," she lashed out. At least she didn't sound like she was about to bawl anymore.

"Fine. Stay in group till you're eighty. I was just trying to help you out," Anthony told her. His arms were itching to cross themselves over his chest and block out as much of the Backstreet Boys T-shirt as possible, but he didn't want to give Rae the satisfaction. How could he have forgotten to turn the T-shirt inside out when he left the house? He'd had to wear it—his little sister would have had hysterics if he hadn't because it was her birthday present to him. But he hadn't meant to actually be seen in it.

"Sorry," Rae muttered, surprising him. He'd have bet she didn't even know the word. She met his gaze directly, and he realized that they were almost exactly the same height. At least she wasn't taller. "And thanks, I guess," she continued. "But you're wrong about school."

"Ten dollars," Anthony said.

"What?" Rae asked.

"Ten dollars says *you're* wrong," Anthony told her. "You can pay up at the next session."

Chapter 2

*S*omebody'll *probably ask if they gave you electric shock.* Rae shook her head as she rinsed the conditioner out of her hair. She twisted the hot water knob to the right until the shower was as hot as she could possibly stand it.

Loofah. She needed the loofah. She reached up and snagged it off the little ledge under the high bathroom window, then squirted on a line of her new bath gel and started to scrub her shoulders.

Somebody'll probably ask if they gave you electric shock.

Rae scrubbed harder, straining to reach the center of her back. She'd already washed her hair three times and conditioned it twice. She pushed down on the loofah, really working it.

Somebody'll probably ask if they gave you electric shock. She could feel the thick fibers of the loofah doing their job. *Use some muscle,* she ordered herself, grinding the loofah into her skin.

More gel. That's what she needed for truly flawless skin. She grabbed the tube and positioned the loofah underneath it. "Oh God," she whispered. "Oh my God." The loofah was streaked with blood. She could even see tiny pieces of skin caught in the fibers.

Rae's knees buckled, and she sat down hard on the tile floor of the shower. She rocked back and forth as the water turned from hot to ice cold. *How could I have done that to myself?* she thought. It was . . . insane. A new kind of insane. She'd really hurt herself. And if she could do that—Rae forced herself to complete the thought. If she could do that, she could do anything. What if next time she picked up a razor blade instead of a loofah?

"It would be better than what happened to Mom," Rae whispered. "I can't live the rest of my life in a hospital. I won't."

A knock came on the bathroom door. "I'll be out in a minute, Dad," she called, her voice cracking.

"It's not Dad. It's Yana. And I have Krispy Kreme doughnuts."

Get it together, Rae, she ordered herself. Yana

Savari was a friend. Sort of. She'd been a volunteer at the hospital. And even though she and Yana were almost the same age and everything, volunteer-patient friendship wasn't exactly a friendship. If Yana saw her in crack-up mode, she'd probably report it to Rae's doctor. For Rae's own good.

Rae scrubbed her face with her hands. Then she used the slick, wet wall of the shower for balance as she struggled to her feet. "One sec, Yana," she called. She pulled in a deep breath, then stepped out of the shower and dried off as quickly as she could, wincing when the towel touched her tender back. "One sec," she called again. She slipped on her cotton robe, then opened the door.

Yana held up the box of doughnuts and grinned. "I remembered how you were always talking about them at the walnut farm."

Rae gave a semihysterical snort of laughter. *Get it together,* she told herself again. "You dyed your hair," she blurted out.

"You like?" Yana asked, holding up a few of her newly pale blond strands.

"I like," Rae answered. "It makes your eyes look even bluer." *Good job, Rae. Very normal sounding,* she thought. She tightened the belt on her robe. "I can't believe you came all the way over here to bring me doughnuts."

"It's not that far," Yana answered. "And I figured we could both use a pre-first-day-of-school sugar rush. I'm on split session, so I don't have to be at my school until noon."

"Um, thanks," Rae said.

"You look shocked to see me," Yana commented.

It *was* pretty freaky to see Yana standing in Rae's hallway, underneath the fluffy white clouds Rae'd painted on the blue walls when she was twelve. "I sort of thought when we did the number-and-address-exchange thing, you might just be being nice to the psycho girl," Rae admitted.

"I'm not that nice. And you're not that psycho," Yana answered. She smiled, showing the little gap between her front teeth. "But you're late. Your dad let me in on the way out, and he made me swear I'd get your butt out the door within the hour. I'm thinking clothes, then—" Yana gave the Krispy Kreme box a shake. "Do you already know what you're going to wear?"

"Yeah. I spent a massive amount of hours last night deciding," Rae confessed. "And what did I choose? Khakis and a button-down shirt, which was the first thing I tried on."

"A little boring for my taste," Yana said. She ran her hand down her Grateful Dead T-shirt, the one she'd cropped to show off the DNA-strand tattoo that

44

circled her belly button. "But perfectly acceptable."

"The kitchen's through the living room. You can hang there while I get ready. Have some coffee or whatever," Rae said as she started down the hallway toward her bedroom.

"Oh my God," Yana exclaimed. "Rae, what hap pened?"

Rae turned around "What?"

"Your back." Yana's eyes were wide with alarm. "It's bleeding."

Rae froze. *I can't go back to the hospital. Can't, can't, can't.*

"I must have, um, cut myself on the edge of the shower door," she blurted out. "It's really sharp."

Yana hurried over to her. "Let me look at it." Before Rae could stop her, Yana circled behind Rae and pulled down the back of her robe. "Ouch," she said softly.

Silence stretched out between them. Rae's heart was pounding so hard, she wouldn't be surprised if Yana could hear it.

"This doesn't look like a cut," Yana finally said. "It looks like a layer of skin was . . . *scraped* off." She pulled Rae's robe back up. "What really happened?"

Rae turned to face her. Yana's serious expression made it clear that another lie wasn't going to cut it.

"I was really nervous, about going back to school,

you know, post- . . . everything. I got obsessed with wanting to look perfect." Rae's voice started to tremble. "I was just . . . I wanted to get off a layer of dead skin. I really didn't mean to hurt myself. Really. You've got to believe me. I just—"

"Got a little overzealous with the exfoliator?" Yana supplied.

"Loofah," Rae said. She gave several quick blinks because her eyes were suddenly feeling wet. "It was an accident. You're not going to tell Dr. Warriner, are you? I can't go back to the hospital, Yana. Please—"

"God, do you think I'm here as some kind of spy?" Yana interrupted. "I finished my hours of community service. Which, by the way, I was assigned to do by the court. The doctors didn't think it would be good for the patients to know that little tidbit."

"The court?" Rae repeated, feeling kind of dazed.

"Frat party. Many cups of lethal punch. Much stupidity. Long story," Yana answered. "Do you have any Bactine? I want to put some on your back."

"Medicine cabinet," Rae answered.

"Go start getting ready." Yana waved her off, then headed back toward the bathroom. Rae stared after her for a long moment, then turned and walked down the hall to her room. On autopilot, she began to get dressed. Yana hurried into the room right as Rae was zipping up her pants.

"Just pretend you're at the gym," Yana said as Rae grabbed a towel to cover her chest. "Turn around."

Rae obeyed. She focused her eyes on the wall across from her. She'd painted it herself, going for a faux marble look in a deep green with black swirls.

"It's not really that bad," Yana told her as she sprayed the cool Bactine on Rae's back. "It's already stopped bleeding."

"But what kind of a nut bucket does that to herself?" Rae muttered. She patted her back with the towel to dab away any remaining blood and Bactine.

"I don't want to hear you call yourself that again," Yana said, her voice harsh. "They let you out of the hospital because you're okay. You're just stressed out this morning."

"You sound like my dad," Rae said as she put on her favorite lacy lavender bra and then gingerly shrugged on her lavender shirt. "Except I actually half believe you," she added, turning to face Yana.

Yana opened the Krispy Kreme box and held it out to Rae. Rae picked a chocolate-glazed old-fashioned. Yana grabbed a cinnamon twist. "You don't believe your dad?" Yana asked. She plopped down on Rae's bed and ran her fingers over the green bedspread with the black diamonds.

"You've got to know my dad. He's this English professor—early stuff, like medieval; you know,

Arthurian legends," Rae said. She pulled the black leather chair away from her desk, a couple of the strange thoughts flashing through her brain, and sat down on the edge of the seat. "He's just not all that well acquainted with reality. We don't even have a TV. And you should hear him talk about my mother. He—"

Rae snapped her mouth shut. She'd almost told Yana the thing she'd spent her whole life trying to keep a secret. And not just a piece of it. The whole ball o' wax.

"He what?" Yana asked.

Rae felt like her ribs were pushing together, digging into her heart. "Nothing," she mumbled.

"Come on." Yana brushed some cinnamon off her chin. "You have to tell me now. You can't get that far and stop. It's against the friendship code."

It might actually feel good to tell her, Rae thought suddenly.

You really are insane, she told herself. *What? You have so many friends right now that you can afford to scare one away?*

But Yana hadn't freaked when she'd seen Rae's back. And she knew Rae'd been at the walnut farm, and that didn't stop her from coming over with doughnuts.

"Come on, Rae," Yana urged.

It's not the same as it was with Lea, Rae thought. *I would have been handing Lea a weapon that she could*

48

have used to make everyone at school think I was a freak. But I've more than taken care of that myself.

Rae swallowed hard, her throat feeling as dry and scratchy as an emery board. "Okay. My mom, she did something really terrible to someone." She swallowed again, realizing that she couldn't do this—couldn't spill what she'd worked so hard to keep secret. Not yet.

"Trust me—it was awful," she continued. "So bad that she would have gone to prison, except she was found mentally unfit to stand trial. She died in a mental institution," Rae said in a rush. "And my dad . . . Anytime he talks about my mother, which isn't that often, he goes on and on about what a great person she was. He totally believes it. That's the sick part. He's not just trying to make me feel better."

"Wow," Yana said softly.

"Yeah." Rae turned her doughnut over and over in her fingers. "So, anyway, you can see why I don't exactly believe everything he says."

Yana pointed at the doughnut. "Eat," she ordered. Rae obediently took a bite. She kept shooting little glances at Yana's face. Was she wondering if Rae was just like her mother? Was she repulsed to be sitting so close to her?

"I never believe anything my dad says, either," Yana commented, her tone matter-of-fact. "But that's probably because he's always telling me how stupid I am. And how lazy. And how unreliable. Isn't that just a pretty, pretty picture?"

"That's awful," Rae said.

Yana stood up. "Yeah, well, in a couple of years we'll both be father-free. Or at least we won't have to live in the same house with them anymore." She pointed at the chunky shoes positioned neatly next to Rae's closet. "Now, put those on. I'm driving you to school. I promised Daddy darling you wouldn't be late, remember?"

The bell rang. Rae knew she had to stand up. She knew she had to head down to the cafeteria. But she felt like all the bones had been surgically removed from her legs. How could she stand up when she had no leg bones? She busied herself putting her English book and her binder into her backpack, not-her thoughts popping in her brain like carbonation in soda as the rest of the class hurried out, laughing, talking, and shooting fast little I'm-not-looking glances at her.

"Rae, would you mind doing us a favor?"

Rae jerked up her head and saw Mr. Jesperson, her English teacher, standing in front of her. Next to him was a guy she didn't recognize—which was probably why he was actually meeting her eye.

"This is Jeff Brunner," Mr. Jesperson continued. "He's new, and he needs someone to show him to the cafeteria. Since it's my first day here, too, I don't think I should be playing tour guide just yet." He gave her a sympathetic smile, a smile that told her he'd already picked up the 411 on her in the teachers' lounge. He probably thought it would be easier for her to return to the scene of the "incident" if she had someone with her. Which was so not true.

"Um, sure. I'll show him," Rae answered because it would be too weird to say no. And without consciously deciding to stand, she was on her feet and leading the way to the door. She pulled it open.

/I CAN'T BELIEVE RAE CAME BACK /went psycho/

God, it was bad enough just getting random thoughts. But these ones were so personal. Having them rush through her brain, with all that static underneath, was like getting attacked from the inside. And they felt so *real*—like they were actually coming from the people around her.

"Thanks for doing this," Jeff said as they stepped into the hall.

"Actually, the cafeteria is incredibly easy to find," she answered. "You know where the main office is, right?" She forced herself to look up at him, and he nodded. "Well, you just follow the mural that starts by the office. It ends right in front of the caf."

"You're not coming?" Jeff asked, his gray eyes all puppy dog. He was cute and possibly trying to flirt, but she was far from flirt mode right now.

"No, I am. Just not right this second." The thought of walking back into the cafeteria was making her dizzy with anxiety.

"Oh. Okay. So, I guess I'll see you around," Jeff said. And he actually blushed. His skin was so fair that the splotches of color looked almost painted on. He gave a half wave and started to stride away from her.

"Wait," she called. He immediately stopped and turned around. "Look. You're new. So you don't know. Although I'm sure you will soon enough." Jeff raised his eyebrows, clearly puzzled. Rae hurried on. "Anyway, last spring I had this kind of meltdown in front of pretty much everyone. Trust me, you don't want to go into the cafeteria with me. You'd be a freak by association." She made a little pushing motion with her hands. "Go on. I'll give you a head start."

Jeff smiled and took a step closer to her. "You're trying to protect me?" He combed his dark hair away from his face with his fingers. "I don't care what people think," he said. "Let's go together."

Wow. The guy had guts, at least. Every new kid knew that who you're seen with those first few days is crucial to your rep.

It would definitely be nice not to have to walk into the cafeteria alone. Those first few seconds, when everyone realized she was there and got all quiet—it wouldn't suck to have someone normal standing next to her.

"Fine," Rae said. She started down the hall without another word. Jeff stayed in step beside her. The hallway had less and less air the closer they got to the cafeteria. She felt like she had to gasp for each breath, although, reality check, she knew she was breathing in a normal way. Which was her goal for the day—breathe normal, walk normal, talk normal, *be* normal.

"Well, here we are," Rae announced, feeling like she had to force the words out of her mouth. She straightened her shoulders, then pushed open the cafeteria's double doors with both hands—

*/gross/see Rae/*gym next period/

—and stepped inside. The volume on the noise went up a notch, then dropped to near silence. Rae didn't think it would be paranoid to attribute the change to her entrance. Her body felt hot all over from all the eyes that were focused on her.

"So this is the cafeteria," Jeff commented.

Rae scanned the room for her friends, spotting Marcus, paying for a slice of pizza. Her stomach clenched in fear at the same time that her heart rate zoomed. She'd spent so much time imagining this moment—seeing him again. But she had no idea what he'd been thinking, what he expected to happen between them now that she was back.

You're supposed to be acting normal, Rae reminded herself. And normal meant her and Marcus, together. It's not like they could just pick up right where they left off, but if she made sure he knew she was better now, that she still wanted to be with him . . .

"I'll be back in one sec," Rae told Jeff. She raced over to Marcus, wrapped one arm around his waist, and pressed her free hand over his eyes. "Guess who?"

"Could it be . . . Dori?" Marcus asked, his voice teasing.

Rae's hand slithered off Marcus's face. "That would be no," she answered, the words coming out a little choked.

What did you expect? she asked herself, her stomach churning with acid. *Did you expect Marcus freaking Salkow to ignore the existence of all other girls for an entire summer?*

Maybe she just hadn't let herself think about that. But she *had* at least figured Lea would give her a heads up if he was seeing someone else.

Marcus turned around. Rae thought she caught a flicker of disgust in his expression, but then he gave her the Salkow smile, his teeth gleaming white against the tan he'd acquired over the summer.

"Sting Rae! You're back," he exclaimed, then wrapped her in a fast hug. Too fast. Like he didn't want to touch her for too long. Like she might be contagious. The acid in her stomach splashed up into the back of her throat.

Get over yourself, Rae thought. *It's just weird for him. Awkward. That's all.*

"Come on," Marcus urged. "Everyone wants to see you."

Rae hadn't gotten the chance to buy food yet, but she followed Marcus toward the usual table. "Jeff, you want to come?" she called over her shoulder. He was standing where she'd left him, his hands shoved awkwardly in his jeans pockets.

"Sure," he answered. In about two seconds he'd caught up to her and Marcus. Rae put her hand lightly on Jeff's arm. "Marcus, this is Jeff. He's new this year."

"Hey," Marcus said. He grabbed Rae by the wrist and started walking faster, tugging her along with him. Jeff kept right up with them.

Good. It wouldn't hurt Marcus—and everyone else who was still staring at her—to see a guy look at her in that she's-hot way, not in the did-you-hear-she-spent-the-summer-in-a-nuthouse way.

"Lea, look who I found!" Marcus called when they'd almost reached the same table they'd always sat at last year.

Lea let out a whoop the second she saw Rae. She sprang off the bench and gave Rae one of those long, rocking hugs, her smooth black hair pressing into

Rae's cheek. "It's so great to see you," she said as she finally released Rae.

"Hey, I think you grew a little upstairs," Rae said softly.

"Yeah, I might actually start having to wear a bra," Lea answered. And for that moment it was as if Rae'd stepped back in time to B.C., before crack-up.

"It's the Rae of sunshine!" Jackie called from the other side of the table. Her voice came out a little too loud and a little too high, but she was trying. And that counted.

"It's the Rae man," Vince bellowed from his seat next to Jackie. "She's back!" Vince sounded like regular Vince. Rae knew he was totally glad to see her. The nice thing about Vince, which was also sometimes the annoying thing about Vince, was that he was a no-subtext kind of guy.

"Sit down," Lea urged, twisting the long chain of beadwork daisies she wore around her neck.

"I actually didn't get food yet," Rae answered.

"I'll do it. I know everything you like." Lea turned toward the food counter.

"Wait," Rae said. "Take Jeff with you." Rae pointed to him and noticed he was starting to blush again. It was actually kind of sweet. "He doesn't have food, either. And he's new. So be nice to him."

"Aren't I always nice to cute boys?" Lea asked.

She grabbed Jeff by the arm and whisked him away. Rae sat down next to Marcus. Then wished she hadn't. Until she figured out what his deal was, she didn't want to look too eager or like she was assuming too much. How humiliating would that be?

"So, Rae, what classes do you have this semester?" Jackie asked. She leaned across the table and patted Rae's hand. Actually *patted* her hand.

"I bet you're doing art again," Vince jumped in before Rae could answer. "You're really great at that." He grinned at her, and she noticed he'd gotten the chip in his tooth fixed. How many other things had changed while she'd been gone?

"Rae's an awesome artist," Marcus added. He glanced nervously over his shoulder.

Rae followed his gaze and saw Dori Hernandez heading toward them. Dori had completely done the caterpillar-to-butterfly thing over the summer. She'd always been cute, but now—complete eye candy. Her long, dark brown hair now fell almost to her waist, and her midriff-baring top showed that she'd lost the few pounds of baby fat she'd been toting around. But what Rae really noticed was how often Dori's eyes darted to Marcus.

A lump the size of a plum formed in Rae's throat. She swallowed hard, then plastered a smile on her face. There was going to be no scene in the cafeteria today. "Hey, Dori. You look great," she said as Dori reached the table.

How long did it take you to make your move? Rae wondered. *A week? A month? Or did you go for it the second after I had my little fit? Did you comfort Marcus about his poor, sick girlfriend?*

"Um, thanks," Dori finally answered, a deer-in-the-headlights expression on her face. She glanced from the empty seat by Rae to the empty seat on the other side of Marcus, shifting uneasily from foot to foot. Marcus finally put her out of her misery by patting the seat next to him.

"Rae was just going to tell us what classes she's taking," Marcus said.

"Oh, great!" Dori cried, sounding like she'd just won an all-expense-paid trip to Hawaii.

"It's just the usual. You know, English, history, bio, gym, trig, plus art, of course," Rae answered.

"Oh, great!" Dori cried again.

Oh, please, Rae thought.

"One Rae Voight special," Lea called as she hurried up to the table with Jeff trailing behind her. She slid a tray in front of Rae. It had one jumbo fro-yo and a salad.

"Thanks," Rae said.

"You're extremely welcome," Lea answered. "Oh, you need napkins," she added. She grabbed a handful

out of the holder in the center of the table and thrust
them on Rae's tray.

Oh God, Rae thought. *Is this how it's going to be
forever? Is everyone going to keep being all fake and
nice, like I'm some kind of severely challenged child
visiting the school?*

She picked up her plastic spoon—
/can Rae tell I'm weirded/

—and scooped up some yogurt. *At least no one
asked me if I've had electric shock*, she thought. *But
I'm definitely going to owe that Anthony guy his ten
bucks.*

* * *

*Rae isn't the kind of girl who finds it easy to trust people.
Maybe she did before her breakdown, but now she's got a
wall around her. I'm not worried. I know I can make her trust
me. I've already made a start. Soon I'll know the truth about
Rachel Voight. And then it will be time to decide what needs
to be done with her.*

Chapter 3

English first period, Anthony thought as he slammed his locker shut, then started out of the building. The perfect way to start the day. His class was over in the row of trailers behind the baseball diamond. Fillmore High had run out of space sometime in the seventies, and the trailers were supposed to be a short-term solution. Yeah, right.

"Yo, fat 'n' smelly," a voice called as he headed outside. Anthony didn't even have to look to know who it was. Brian Salerno was the only guy who still called Anthony by his grade-school nickname. Salerno was also the only guy who still actually thought the fact that Fascinelli sounded sort of like "fat 'n' smelly" was freakin' HBO-comedy-special material.

"Hey," Anthony said. He didn't slow down as

Salerno fell into step beside him. He wondered if there was a possibility that by the time they graduated, whatever millennium that might be, Salerno would figure out that not only weren't they friends, but that they had never *been* friends.

"So you in Goyer's class?" Salerno asked as they cut across the baseball field.

"Yeah." They reached the trailer, and Anthony climbed up the flimsy aluminum steps, then pulled open the door. The metal was warm under his hand, and it wasn't even ten in the morning. He stepped inside and immediately spotted a lot of familiar faces. "Bluebirds," he muttered.

No one was called Bluebirds, Canaries, or Cardinals anymore, but they were still the friggin' Bluebirds all right. And everybody knew it. Just like back in the third grade no one had had a problem breaking their teacher's little reading-group code. Bluebirds equaled morons.

The second bell rang. Goyer stood up from behind her desk and wrote her name on the board. "I'm Ms. Goyer. Welcome back to school. I hope you all had a great summer." She smiled as she picked up a stack of paper, then handed sets of stapled-together sheets to the first kid in every row. "After I call roll, we're going to do a little reading aloud. Just to ease you back into the routine."

Just to see who are the biggest Bluebirds of them all, Anthony thought as the girl in front of him passed back his set of papers. He shifted in his hard wooden chair. Dots of sweat had popped out all the way down the groove in the center of his back, and they were itching like crazy. He checked the clock. Not even two minutes of class time had elapsed, and the second hand was moving in extreme slow motion.

Anthony stretched his legs out into the aisle. He clenched and unclenched his fingers. *Relax, okay? Freakin' relax,* he told himself. He gave a "yo" when Ms. Goyer called his name, not bothering to return her bright you're-so-special smile. Goyer was clearly one of those special-ed teachers who was sure a little love and attention would get all her Bluebirds in the air, flying like Cardinals. Which was slightly easier to take than the special-ed teachers who thought all a Bluebird needed was to have its feathers plucked so it would learn a little discipline. Slightly.

Mental porn. That's the only way he was going to get through. *Girl from the Gap ad,* he decided. *The redhead. Yeah.* She came so clear in his mind that he could see every freckle.

"Okay, you take it from there, Anthony," Goyer called in her all-they-need-is-a-little-encouragement voice. It took him a second to bring the sheet of paper on his desk back into focus.

Both armpits started pumping juice. The trickle of sweat down his back turned into a stream, gluing his T-shirt to his skin. *Get a grip,* he ordered himself. *It's reading a few sentences.*

"Mike," Anthony read. That was an easy one. A picture of his friend Mike flashed into his head as soon as his eyes hit the letters, so he instantly recognized the word. *Ran.* As soon as Anthony had pictured himself running, the word had easily come out of his mouth. He moved his eyes to the next word—*to.* One of his heels started slapping up and down on the floor. "To," he said. He'd actually had to think about that one. Two letters and he'd had to think about it.

Anthony moved on to the next word—*the.* Another word that didn't bring up any kind of picture. *But you know it,* he told himself. *It's one of the easy ones. It's one of the ones kids still in diapers know.* He intensified his focus. "The," he said.

"Good. Keep going," Goyer urged.

Anthony didn't look up from the sheet. He couldn't lose his concentration. "Store," he said. That hadn't been a problem. He'd seen the word, and a picture of the grocery store near his house had popped into his head, but he got blank brain again on the next word—*and.* He focused until he felt like a steel belt was wrapped around his head, getting pulled tighter and tighter. "And," he read.

He wished whoever was chewing gum would stop it. The sweet grape smell was making him nauseous. And somebody else was gnawing on a pencil, which made his teeth want to crawl right out of his mouth.

"Try sounding it out," Ms. Goyer prompted.

Anthony jerked his eyes to the next word. The image of him handing money to his pot dealer appeared in his mind "Bought," he said. He moved his eyes to the next word. No picture. "Some," he managed to get out.

The belt around his head cinched tighter. His foot tapped harder against the floor. The smell of grape gum felt like it was filling his nose and throat and lungs. And his teeth were practically jumping with each crunch of the pencil from the other side of the room.

"Why don't you start again at the beginning," Ms. Goyer suggested.

Anthony put his finger under the first word of the sentence. He knew it made him look like a goon, but it helped. An image of his friend Mike appeared in his mind. "Mike," he said. He moved his finger to the next word. An image of Anthony running appeared. "Ran." He moved his finger to the next word. His mind went blank again.

"Sound it out," Ms. Goyer said. "What is the sound of the first letter?"

Anthony dug his finger into the paper under the

word. The little two-letter word. He pulled in a deep breath, a sweet, grape-scented breath that made him want to gag.

"Mike ran to the girl with the humongous melon breasts," Anthony said in a rush, half under his breath. He cut a glance at Goyer. She didn't look angry. She had an aw-poor-little-Bluebird-acting-out expression on her face.

"We'll go over some techniques for attacking unfamiliar words next class," she said. "Brian, continue, please."

Anthony checked the clock again. They'd just about hit the halfway mark. But he needed out of here *now*. He called the Gap redhead up in his mind again and made her unbutton her sweater. She slipped it from her shoulders and let it fall to her feet in a pink puddle. *Yeah.*

When he got tired of Red, he switched over to one of the blond chicks from the ad. Blondie kept him occupied until the bell rang. Then he was out of there. He broke into a run as he cut across the baseball diamond, loving the way his muscles obeyed his slightest command, the way his crammed-with-stupid brain never would. Man, he couldn't wait for gym. That was the one place *he* was the Cardinal. No, forget that. He was the Eagle.

But gym wasn't until last period. Next up was

math. Bluebird math. *At least it's not in the trailer park,* he thought as he headed into the main building and started toward his locker. He hesitated when he passed the pay phone. He shouldn't have to do this . . . but he'd bet anything his mom had forgotten. He turned back toward the phone, pulled a quarter out of the pocket of his jeans, dropped it in the slot, and dialed a number.

"Sunny Days Day Care," a voice that sounded a lot like Ms. Goyer's answered.

"This is Anthony Fascinelli," he said. "Carl Doheney's brother. Carl's on antibiotics. He needs to take a pill at lunch with food, okay? The pills are in his backpack." He hung up without waiting for a reply and continued toward his locker. At least now he wouldn't have to listen to Carl screaming all night because his earache hurt so bad. Something you'd think the kid's own mother would care about.

"Mr. Fascinelli," a familiar voice called. Way too familiar.

He turned around. "Mr. Shapiro. Hi! I hope you had a fabulous summer," Anthony said with mock enthusiasm. He couldn't believe this. First Bluebird English *with* reading aloud. Now a chat with the principal. He bet that girl from group's first day at school was a walk in the park compared to this.

Shapiro didn't look amused. His muddy green

eyes were all squinty, and his thin lips looked even thinner because he had them pressed together so tight.

"I got an update on you from your group therapy leader at Oakvale," Mr. Shapiro said. "It looks like you're making some progress in your anger management skills. I expect to see some evidence of that this year."

Anthony nodded. Clearly he wasn't expected to say anything here.

"I'm giving you fair warning," Mr. Shapiro continued. "One step out of line this year and there's no second chance. You're out of here."

Anthony nodded again. It was a better anger management choice than slamming his fist into the closest wall. He'd learned that much. But what was the guy's friggin' problem? Anthony hadn't done anything. *Anything.* And Shapiro was already busting his butt. Nice welcome to his junior year.

"You better head off," Shapiro said. "You don't want to be late to class your first day."

"I sure don't," Anthony answered, unable to keep the sarcasm out of his voice. He strode past Shapiro, getting in a little shoulder knock that could possibly have been an accident. Then instead of going to his locker, he swung into the bathroom. He couldn't deal with another class right now.

Anthony ducked into the closest stall, opened his

backpack, and then pulled a plastic bag out of one of the zippered compartments. Just holding the bag in his hand made his heart rate go down and loosened the belt around his head.

He rolled himself a joint as quickly as he could. *Yeah,* he thought as he took the first toke and held the smoke in his lungs, *now this is the way to start the first day of school.* He heard the bathroom door swing open, and he checked the lock on his stall to make sure it was in place.

"Someone has been using that wacky tobaccy in here," a voice said.

"And *somebody* better be willing to share," another voice added. "That means you, Fascinelli."

A second later Gregg Borgenicht's head popped over the left side of Anthony's stall, followed almost immediately by Mike Tarcher's on the right. "Gimme, gimme, gimme," Gregg begged. He sounded like a little kid. And with his round face he looked kind of like one, too. Even with the scraggly goatee.

Anthony took another pull before he handed Gregg the joint. Who knew when he'd get it back. But he was glad to see the guys. Smoking with them was definitely more fun than smoking alone. They always managed to crack him up.

"We have to ask Anthony our question," Mike told Gregg.

"Definitely," Gregg answered, speaking with his lips almost closed so he wouldn't lose any smoke. Although clearly he was already at least partially in his special happy place, going by the red eyes, eyes with pupils so big, they almost blocked out the blue.

"So, okay. Say the world was made of cheese," Gregg said. He looped his elbows over the edge of Anthony's stall, probably to keep his balance on the lidless toilet seat he had to be standing on. "What do you think money would be? I say crackers. Because hey, with cheese you gotta have crackers. But to Mike money would be—" Gregg paused since it was his turn to suck, then continued, his voice thick. "He thinks money would be Dr. Pepper."

"Because Dr. Pepper is great with cheese," Mike cut in. "You just can't eat cheese without Dr. Pepper." He reached for the joint with his long, skinny fingers. Gregg started to hand it to him, but Anthony intercepted. It *was* his last one.

Anthony gave a bark of laughter. "Why wouldn't money still be money, geniuses?" he asked. "Then people could buy Dr. Pepper or crackers or whatever they wanted to go with the cheese."

Gregg snorted. "You're not getting it, *genius*. The world . . . It's *made* of cheese. That changes everything. Everything! People wouldn't still be walking around with, like, quarters."

"Yeah, 'cause there would be no metal to make into quarters," Mike added, fingering the scattered hair on his chin. "There'd be, like, veins of Cheez Whiz that you could lap right up."

Anthony took another toke while he tried to imagine Cheese World. He'd bet anything Rae and her prep school friends didn't have conversations like this. They probably only talked about what college they were planning to go to—with Mommy and Daddy's money.

"So are the buildings made out of cheese, too?" Anthony asked, already starting to feel nice 'n' fuzzy.

"Cheese would have to be the main construction material," Gregg answered.

"Maybe peanut butter could be the mortar. Like in those crackers at the 7-Eleven," Mike suggested.

"I love those crackers," Anthony said. He smiled as he thought about them. So orange. So crunchy.

"But peanut butter is the mortar between *crackers* in those things. It's not the mortar between pieces of *cheese*," Gregg told Mike, sounding annoyed. "What are you thinking?"

"Would you keep it down?" Anthony said. "We don't want Shapiro joining the party."

"I really want some of those crackers," Mike murmured. "Time for a 7-Eleven run. You comin'?" he asked Anthony.

Anthony scrubbed his face with his fingers,

almost burning one eyebrow with the joint. "I gotta go to my next class," he said. "I already missed one."

"We all already missed one." Mike snagged the joint. "But what we do is leave now, then come back at lunch, when we can blend."

And I could score another bag from Rick, Anthony thought. He was probably working today. And if he wasn't, he was probably hanging out in the 7-Eleven parking lot so all his regulars could find him.

"So are you comin' or what?" Gregg asked.

Anthony checked Gregg's watch. There was no way he could get back in time for Bluebird history. It's not like he wanted to sit through another hour of torture, but he did want to graduate so that someday the torture would end. If he hung out too much with Gregg and Mike, that wasn't going to happen. Gregg had already been held back a year.

"Can't do it," Anthony said. "But get me some of those peanut butter crackers. And don't eat them on the way back," Anthony ordered Mike, then handed him the money. Mike and Gregg each gave him a half salute and disappeared from sight. The door swung shut behind them before Anthony realized that Mike had made off with his last doobie.

Just as well, Anthony told himself. *You don't want to become a walking baked potato like those guys.* He sat down on the edge of the toilet. *Yeah, no more pot*

*for you, young man. Not until there's a four-day week-
end or something. You've got to graduate. Otherwise
you'll end up here for the rest of your friggin' life. Or
working at the 7-Eleven, selling munchies to Gregg
and Mike.*

And I am outta here, Anthony thought as he
headed through Fillmore's main doors. Just a couple
dozen steps and he'd be off school property, at least
until tomorrow. He started walking faster, then stopped
short when he saw Rick Nunan leaning against one of
the two oak trees that dominated the front of the
school. Rick had already spotted him, so there was no
point in Anthony pretending he hadn't seen the guy.

"Knew you had to be down to the seeds," Nunan
said as Anthony approached. "Since you're one of my
very special customers and all, I decided to make a
delivery."

Translation: You needed some fast cash, Anthony
thought. Nunan was an okay guy. They'd partied
together. But he wasn't a doing-it-out-of-the-
goodness-of-his-heart type. Not by a long shot.

"Gonna have to pass," Anthony answered.

"You broke? I can spot you for a few days." Nunan
ran his fingers over his shaved head. When he was
high, just the feel of the skin under his fingers could
make him giggle for hours.

"Nah. I just . . ." Anthony shrugged. "Not in the mood." Which was total crap. But he'd ordered himself not to buy any more. He was going to graduate from this place without taking ten freaking years to do it.

"Not in the mood?" Nunan repeated. "You smoke some, you get in the mood." He ran his hand over his head again.

"Just go find one of your other very special customers, okay?" Anthony asked. *And right now,* he added to himself. His fingers were already twitching, ready to go for his wallet.

Nunan took a step closer, and Anthony was blasted with the smell of smoke.

"It's totally primo stuff. Nunan tested, Nunan approved."

Anthony didn't think. He just reacted—by reaching out and shoving Nunan away with both hands. Nunan, the little weenie, ended up on his butt.

"Is there a problem, Mr. Fascinelli?" a voice called. Anthony glanced over his shoulder. Oh, friggin' perfect. Mr. Shapiro *had* to have seen that little encounter. And his lips were clamped together so tight, they'd practically disappeared into his mouth.

"No problem." Anthony reached down, grabbed Nunan's hand, and pulled him up. "No problem, right, Rick?"

"Nonstudents aren't allowed on campus," Shapiro

told Nunan. It took a second for Nunan to realize that meant he should leave, but he finally got it and wandered off.

"I have the feeling you weren't listening to me this morning, Anthony," Shapiro said, opening his mouth only enough to let the words squeak through.

"No, I was. I was," Anthony answered. He hated the way his voice came out, like a little kid's. *Don't be mad, Mommy. I'll never do it again.*

Shapiro nodded. "We'll see, won't we." He turned and walked away without another word.

Perfect end to a perfect day. But at least it's over. And I survived. Wonder if Rae made it out alive from her little prep school.

Chapter 4

"**S**o how was school?" Rae's father asked before she even had her butt all the way into the car.

Rae slammed the door. "Day two was pretty much like day one," she answered. Stares. Extreme niceness. Extreme weirdness. Random not-her-own thoughts about how psycho she was. Plus some totally-her-own thoughts about how psycho she was, just for variety. "You know, just basic getting-organized stuff," she added as her dad pulled out of the driveway.

Whoo-hoo, time to party!

A sour taste filled Rae's mouth. She popped open the glove compartment—

/What am I supposed to say to her?/

—and rooted around for some gum. She didn't

77

find any, so she slammed the glove compartment closed.

/*Rachel*/

God, that thought, it *felt* like her dad. It wasn't in his voice or anything. But it had a Dad . . . *flavor*.

She reminded herself what Dr. Warriner had said when she'd admitted that sometimes the thoughts really seemed to come from other people, especially thoughts *about* her.

That's part of what paranoiac delusions are, Rae. You're imagining that people must be thinking these things of you, and so you're projecting the thoughts onto them—in your own head.

Rae leaned back and rubbed her forehead. *Maybe some sort of exorcism would be useful,* she thought.

"Would you like to stop for a Slurpee on the way?" her father asked.

"No, thanks. Not unless you want one," Rae said. She turned her head toward the window so he couldn't see the film of tears coating her eyes. Would he ever stop *offering* her stuff in that hopeful, eager voice?

"I'm not really a Slurpee person. Although I like the word. *Slurpee. Slurrrpeee.* It's onomatopoetic, don't you think?" her dad asked. "The word *slurp* sounds like the sound that you make when you slurp."

Oh God. He's slipped into educational mode, Rae

thought. She gave a couple of blinks, and her eyes cleared up.

They were still about fifteen minutes away from Oakvale. She was not going to be able to take this. "Dad, what was Mom like when you went to visit her in the hospital?"

Oh my God, she thought. She had so not been intending to ask that. All she'd wanted to do was change the subject, and the Mom question had come spewing out. Rae shot a glance at her dad. He didn't seem upset. He looked like he was giving her question careful consideration.

"She was very much herself," he finally answered. "Although sometimes the medication they had her on made her a little . . . dulled. Your mother, usually she sparkled." He reached out and briefly touched Rae's face. "You sparkle, too, sometimes."

How to sparkle. Step one—go insane, Rae thought. Not an article soon to appear in *Self* magazine.

"We had some wonderful conversations when I would visit," her father continued, his voice the slightest bit thick. "We talked about you a lot, of course. She wanted to know every single detail. Every burp. Every smile. But we'd talk about philosophical questions, too, the way we had when we were dating."

He loved her so much, Rae thought. That was clear every time he talked about her. Every time Rae *let* him talk about her. She knew he'd talk about her more if Rae didn't go into shark-attack mode when he did, reminding him what this goddess had done.

"Did you ever have any sense that something was wrong? Before what happened, I mean," Rae asked. She usually hated talking about her mom. But this was info she needed now.

"No," he answered immediately. "Not really," he added, his words coming slowly. "Except that near the . . . the time, she seemed agitated. She was ecstatic because you had just been born. But I knew she was worried about something. She wouldn't tell me what. She never did, not even afterward, when she was in the hospital."

He shot a glance at Rae, his blue eyes unusually intense. "I think she was protecting me from something. She was like that, always putting other people first."

Rae focused all her attention on adjusting the air-conditioner vent in front of her. If it helped Dad to be delusional, maybe she shouldn't burst his pretty bubble.

"I didn't want to push her. Not when she was in the hospital. I thought there would be plenty of time for her to tell me what was bothering her. But then, a few months after she was institutionalized, she got sick. Her body began to deteriorate. It happened so rapidly that her doctors weren't able to diagnose her before she died," he continued. "And I never got to . . . We never got to really talk again." Her father grabbed his sunglasses off the dashboard and put them on, but not before Rae saw the tears in his eyes. "They wanted to do an autopsy," he continued. "But I wouldn't give them permission. I just . . . I couldn't." Her father wiped his face with the sleeve of his white shirt. Then he pulled onto the exit leading to Oakvale.

"Thanks for telling me," Rae said softly.

"I'll always answer your questions," he said, shooting her a glance. "I *want* you to know about your mother. You would have liked her, Rae. You would have loved her."

Rae adjusted her thin beaded hair band. She and her father fell into a somewhat comfortable silence that lasted until he pulled into Oakvale's parking lot.

"See you in an hour," her dad said. Rae nodded and pulled open the door.

Whoo-hoo, time to party!

That thought again. She'd noticed that some of her not-her thoughts were on a loop or something. They'd come back now and then, but each time they were a little bit fuzzier. Which would be encouraging, except she got new not-her thoughts all the time, and they came in loud and clear.

Rae slammed the car door —

Why is this!

—and hesitated. There was something about that why-is-this one that was more comfortable than a lot of the others. Closer to one of her own thoughts, but not exactly. Actually, the whoo-hoo thought was like that, too. Why? She had no clue.

"So where's my ten bucks?" a voice called from behind her as she headed up to Oakvale's main doors. Rae turned around and saw Anthony striding up, his hand stuck out for his money.

At least he's not NutraSweet nice to me, she thought, *like one wrong word and somebody's going to have to go running for a straitjacket.*

Rae didn't even bother to pretend that Anthony was wrong about school. She just reached into her mesh bag, feeling for her wallet. Before she could find it, Anthony caught her by the wrist, his fingers light but firm.

"You don't have to pay," he told her.

Rae glanced down at her wrist, and Anthony instantly released her. She noticed he wasn't wearing his Backstreet Boys T-shirt today. Just a faded tan T-shirt that made his brown eyes look even darker. It fit a little better, too, showing off some nice definition in the chest and ab areas. Make that very nice.

"Were they completely, uh, hellish? Your first two days?" Anthony muttered, not quite looking Rae in the eye.

Rae snorted. "Well, let's see," she said sarcastically. "To people at school, I'm either this poor thing who can't even eat without someone to wipe her mouth for her. Or I'm this freak who should be avoided in case I might still be contagious with some kind of insanity disease. Even to my friends. Would you call that hellish?"

"That sucks," Anthony said. He managed to briefly look at her. Rae was surprised to see sympathy in his eyes. Not poor-little-Rae pity. Real sympathy.

"Yeah," Rae agreed. "It completely sucks. So what about you? Did you end up puking or anything?"

Anthony gave a harsh laugh. "No, but hanging around with the friggin' Bluebirds all day made me want to."

"Bluebirds?" Rae shook her head. "What are—"

A deep flush started to creep up Anthony's neck. "Slow learners," he muttered. "I have to go take a leak." And he bolted.

All righty, then, Rae thought. *That was a bizarre little exchange. One where I think we actually both told each other the truth—and didn't exactly plan to.* She pushed open half of the double door—

WHAT A MORON!

—and stepped inside. A girl from group, around Rae's age, who looked like she bought all her clothes from an army surplus store, immediately rushed up to her. "I can't believe we're back here again. Can you believe group meets three times a week? It's ridiculous."

"Yeah," Rae agreed. She had the urge to back away a step but didn't. *Is this how I look to people?* she wondered. *All nervous and jittery and about to go off?*

"Hey," the girl said, nervously tickling the side of her neck with the end of her braid. "Your mascara is sort of smudged. Do you know where the bathroom is? It's—"

"I know. Thanks, Cynda," Rae said, finally remembering the girl's name. *Thanks for giving me a great excuse to get away*, Rae added silently as she hurried down the hall. She pushed open the bathroom door—

/TOTAL MORON/

—and almost bumped into Anthony. "Guys' is flooded," he mumbled as he ducked past her.

Whatever, Rae thought. She headed over to the closest mirror and peered in. What was that Cynda girl talking about? Rae's mascara wasn't smudged at all. She leaned on the rust-stained sink—

/never know what hit her/

—to get a closer look. And suddenly a blast shook the floor beneath her feet. Something hard struck the back of Rae's head. She fell to her knees, white dots exploding in front of her eyes.

Dimly she could hear shouts from the hall. But the voices sounded much too far away. And something warm was dripping down her neck. *Blood*, she realized slowly. From her head. She had to get up. Had to get help.

She grabbed the sink with both hands—

/they'll think Anthony did it/definitely kill Rae/get out of here/

—and pulled herself to her feet. Her legs felt soft as marshmallows. She gripped the sink harder so she wouldn't fall again.

/how does this thing/should have brought/definitely kill Rae/

That thought again. Why did she get that thought again? *Definitely kill Rae.* Had someone just tried to kill her?

Anthony jumped out of his metal chair so fast that it crashed to the floor. That explosion—it sounded like it came from the direction of the girls' bathroom. Where Rae was! His body reacted instantly, and he was out the door and down the hall in seconds, then pushing through the bathroom door.

A dozen different pieces of data hit him as soon as he was inside. Stall door blown off. Smell of smoke. Smell of blood. Pieces of broken tile. Rae swaying on her feet in front of the cracked mirror.

Anthony reached her just as her knees buckled and caught her before she hit the floor. He scooped her up, one arm around her shoulders, one under her knees, and carried her out of the bathroom, using his back to open the door. Her face had lost all its color, and her eyes were only slitted open. "I'm taking her to the nurse," he announced as he strode past Ms. Abramson and most of the group.

"Everybody back to the room. And no one goes into that bathroom," Abramson called. A second later she caught up to Anthony. "Rae, can you hear me?" she asked loudly.

Anthony stared down at Rae's face. His stomach turned over as her eyelids fluttered open and she looked directly up at him. "I don't need to be carried," she said. "I'm fine."

"Yeah, right," Anthony answered, not even considering putting her down. What was it with this girl and being helped?

"I'll get the door." Abramson rushed on ahead and jerked open the door to the nurse's office. "Sheila, we need you," she cried, her voice shrill.

When he reached the door, Anthony turned sideways and carefully maneuvered himself and Rae through. The last thing she needed was another bump on the head. He could feel her blood soaking into his T-shirt.

"Put her over there," the nurse ordered, waving toward the closest of three empty cots along the back wall.

"I can walk," Rae protested again, giving a little squirm.

"You can fall on your butt," Anthony answered. He strode over to the narrow cot and carefully laid Rae down on the thin blue blanket. "Don't even think about trying to sit up," he warned her. He backed up to let the nurse move in next to the cot, but he didn't take his eyes off Rae, his gaze locked on the tiny scratch that ran along one side of her face from the top of her cheek to the corner of her mouth.

"Anthony, we've got it covered now," Abramson told him. "You can go back to the meeting room."

He nodded, but he didn't move. He kept thinking there was something he should be doing. Water. He bet Rae would like a drink of water. Anthony scanned the room and spotted a water cooler, then he hurried over to it. He rejected the wimpy paper cups and picked a big blue plastic one off the shelf over the coffeepot. As soon as he got it filled—almost full, but not so full it would be easy for Rae to spill—he rushed back over to the cot.

"Here. I'm leaving this for you." Anthony put the cup on the little table next to Rae. He hesitated a moment, but he couldn't think of anything else she might want, so he headed out.

He could hear the chaos in the meeting room before he was even halfway there.

"Is she okay?" Cynda asked as soon as he stepped back in the room. She gnawed on the end of her braid as she waited for him to answer.

"Yeah," Anthony said. He started toward the closest empty chair but was intercepted by Jesse.

"They're saying it was a pipe bomb," Jesse said, clearly eager to be the one to give Anthony the info.

"Sounds like bull. Who would put a pipe bomb in the girls' bathroom?" Anthony asked. His heart was still beating like crazy, and his body hadn't figured out that it was okay to stop pumping the adrenaline. And the sweat.

"I don't know. But that's what I heard Mr. Rocha saying," Jesse answered. He used his fingers to comb his red hair off his face. "You should have seen him. That little vein by his eye looked like it was about to explode. Rocha's totally out for blood on this one."

Yeah, and I bet I'm on the top of his list, Anthony thought. *If there's trouble, any kind of trouble, who you gonna call? Fascinelli.* Mr. Rocha, the director of the institute, was exactly like Mr. Shapiro in that way.

But this time I'm totally clean, Anthony told himself. *Even if Rocha wants to, he's not going to be able to pin this on me.*

Except for the little fact that Rae saw Anthony coming out of the girls' bathroom. The sweat on his body turned cold. Rae could place him at the scene about two minutes before the bomb went off. If that.

She won't say anything, he told himself. He and Rae weren't friends. Hardly. But she wouldn't— Anthony gave the sleeve of his T-shirt a yank. Rae's blood was starting to glue itself to his arm.

You've known each other for, like, two hours, he thought. *Get real. You have no idea what she is or isn't going to say. Fascinelli, you are totally screwed.*

Chapter 5

"**A**re you feeling okay sitting up?" Mr. Rocha asked Rae. "We can go back to the nurse's office and talk. That way you could keep lying down."

"I'm fine," Rae answered. She lightly touched the bandage on the back of her head—

/good as new/

—and grimaced when she realized a little blood had soaked through.

"You're sure?" Mr. Rocha pressed.

Like you care, Rae thought. She didn't see any real concern in his hazel eyes. And even though it would feel good to lie down again, she did *not* want to have this little chat with Rocha with her in bed and him looming over her. Just too icky.

"I'm fine," Rae repeated.

"You're also very lucky," Mr. Rocha told her, adjusting the crystal paperweight so it was exactly in the center of the stack of papers on his desk. "If you'd been a few feet closer to the bomb when it went off, we wouldn't be talking about whether you're feeling well enough to sit. You'd be in the hospital. Or dead."

"Wait. Bomb? There was a bomb?" Rae demanded.

The not-her thought she'd gotten in the bathroom ripped through her mind. *Definitely kill Rae.* Did that thought actually mean something? Was someone trying to *kill* her?

"A pipe bomb," Mr. Rocha answered. "It was in the stall closest to the door." He leaned across his desk toward her. "What I need to know is, did you see anything unusual in the bathroom?"

Anthony, she thought, her stomach doing a slow-mo flip-flop. That was pretty unusual, seeing a guy coming out of the girls' bathroom.

"I mean *anything,*" Rocha said, a few droplets of spittle flying out of his mouth.

The cut on the back of Rae's head began to throb in time to the beat of her heart. "I don't get it. What's the point of a pipe bomb in the girls' bathroom? Was someone trying to blow up the entire place or what?"

Because that sort of made sense. It's not like people ended up coming to Oakvale because they were *stable.* Maybe one of the squirrels decided that their mission was to send the place to heaven.

Rocha shook his head. "Not unless whoever is responsible severely miscalculated," he answered. "The bomb wasn't big enough to damage more than the bathroom. Now, try to remember everything. Even the smallest detail can help me find the person who did this."

Wonder what he'd think if I told him that I had one of my not-me thoughts in the bathroom? One that said, "Definitely kill Rae." She could just hear herself. *The bomb was set because someone wanted to murder me, Mr. Rocha. Something in my head told me so.* Yeah, that would get her back in the hospital nice and fast. And probably for a lot longer than a summer vacation.

But I'd definitely have been dead if I went into that stall, Rae thought suddenly. A tremor snaked its way through her body. She reached out and grabbed her big cup of water off Rocha's desk.

/SHE'S OKAY/SO PALE/WHAT ELSE COULD I GET FOR HER/

There was something familiar about those thoughts. Like when you heard an announcer on TV and then later realized it was some washed-up celeb.

Kathleen Turner shilling for Burger King or whatever.

"Anything at all, Rachel," Mr. Rocha pressed.

"All I did was walk in and go over to the closest sink," Rae told him. The not-her thoughts kept repeating in her mind, growing slightly fuzzier, not staticky, just softer and not quite as clear.

/SHE'S OKAY/SO PALE/WHAT ELSE COULD I GET FOR HER/

Anthony, she thought suddenly. *They remind me of Anthony.* Which made no sense. Except that when he was carrying her to the nurse's office, he'd looked so scared. Scared for her. The thoughts sort of fit with how he'd been acting.

"I checked my makeup in the mirror. Then—bam! I didn't even realize it was a bomb. I didn't have time to realize anything." Rae knew she should mention Anthony. Seeing him was a lot more than the smallest detail. But in those thoughts . . . It was like Anthony was really worried about her. Like he . . . like he . . . *cared* about her, wanted to help her somehow.

Uh, hello? Psycho girl? Remember Dr. Warriner? Those thoughts in your head didn't come from Anthony. And the ones that sounded like Dad, they didn't come from Dad. And the one about definitely killing Rae, that didn't come from anyone else, either. Believing they did is going to a whole new number on the nutso scale. But still, it was getting harder and harder *not* to feel like the thoughts were real.

"What about people?" Mr. Rocha asked, his flat

hazel eyes intent on Rae's face. "Anyone near the bathroom when you went in?"

There were more not-me thoughts in the bathroom, she remembered. *What were they?* There was one about Anthony. Something like, *They'll think Anthony did it.* Did that mean Anthony was being framed? Because if he was, then she absolutely shouldn't say—

What did you just decide about your freaky thoughts? Rae asked herself. *You decided it would be insane to actually think they mean anything. Now, have you decided to go there? Just take a running dive into the loony bin?*

"Rachel, are you having trouble concentrating?" Mr. Rocha asked. "I'm starting to think that blow to your head was more serious—"

"I was just wondering about my dad," Rae said quickly. "Is someone checking the parking lot for him? I'm sure he went to get coffee or something. Usually he just sits in the car and reads until I'm through."

"Sheila—the nurse—is watching for him. She'll bring him in as soon as he gets here," Mr. Rocha answered. "Now, what about who you saw? Was there anyone?"

Rae shifted her plastic cup from one hand to the other.

/SHE'S OKAY/WHAT ELSE COULD I GET FOR HER/GONNA FIND OUT WHO DID THIS/

God, those thoughts really *did* feel like Anthony, even though they kept getting a little softer, a little *blurrier.*

"Rachel, if you saw someone, you have to tell me. We're talking about a serious crime here," Mr. Rocha said, impatience flaring in his voice.

"Rae. My name's Rae," she told him sharply.

"Fine. Rae. Now, Rae, did you see anyone around the bathroom?" Mr. Rocha asked again. "I'm sure the police will ask you the same question. But it would help me to hear the answer now."

This wasn't going away. She was going to be asked about what happened again and again. So should she lie or what?

Rae put the cup back down on the desk. She just couldn't picture Anthony setting a bomb.

Reality check, she thought. *The guy's not going to group therapy three times a week for nothing. You have no idea how he ended up here or what he would or wouldn't do. Yeah, he was somewhat nice to you, in his own perverse way, but you don't owe him anything.*

She picked up the cup again and—

/SO PALE/WHAT ELSE COULD I GET FOR HER/GONNA FIND OUT WHO DID THIS/

—took a sip, stalling. "I'm just trying to think. Everything is a little jumbled," Rae said. She wished hearing those psycho Anthony-flavored thoughts didn't make her feel all warm inside.

"Take your time," Mr. Rocha said, although she noticed the vein next to his eye had started to pulse.

Rae squeezed her eyes shut for a moment. *You don't really have a choice here,* she thought. She opened her eyes again and met Mr. Rocha's gaze. "When I was going into the bathroom, Anthony was coming out."

"Anthony Fascinelli was in the girls' bathroom?" Mr. Rocha asked eagerly.

Rae nodded. And a spike of pain jammed itself into her head.

Anthony's head jerked to the door as it swung open. Rae walked through. Not quite so pale, he noted. Before, even her lips had been bloodless. Now they were back to their usual deep pink, and there was a little color in her cheeks, too. Anthony felt the muscles in the back of his neck relax a little.

Then he realized that Rocha was right behind Rae and that Rocha's little hazel eyes were locked on him. All Anthony's neck muscles tightened up again. So did the muscles in his shoulders. And the ones all the way down the length of his back. *Rae gave me up,* he thought with a sinking feeling.

"Anthony Fascinelli, please come with me," Rocha ordered, sounding so freakin' pleased with himself. Anthony shot a glance at Rae. She didn't even have the guts to look him in the eye. *Thanks for nothing,* he thought as he grabbed his backpack and headed for the door. He couldn't believe less than an hour ago he'd been having an actual conversation with that girl. Telling her about the friggin' *Bluebirds* and everything.

"Now," Rocha added. Anthony stumbled to his feet and followed Rocha down the hall in silence, his mind racing around like a greyhound on a track.

What am I going to tell him? Anthony thought. *I can't go with the story about the guys' bathroom being flooded. Way too easy to check out. And it's not like I can tell him the truth.*

Yeah, Anthony could just see himself sitting in that hard chair across from Rocha and explaining what happened.

See, my pot dealer, my former pot dealer, is an idiot. Even though just yesterday I told him I didn't want to buy any more dope from him, I get this message that he decided to do me a favor and leave some for me taped under the toilet in the last stall of the girls' bathroom. I did mention he's an idiot, right? Anyway, I had to go get it because I was afraid the genius wrote my name on it or something. I'd show you the pot, you know, to back my story up. But I flushed it. You believe that, don't you, Mr. Rocha? It's written all over your files that Anthony Fascinelli is a total pothead. But you believe I've changed, right?

No, that definitely wouldn't cut it, Anthony thought. They reached Rocha's office, and Rocha held open the door for him with exaggerated politeness.

Anthony knew the drill. He sat down in the wooden chair while Rocha circled around and plopped his butt down on the padded chair behind the desk.

"Rachel Voight told me she saw you coming out of the girls' bathroom. Want to tell me what you were doing in there?" Rocha demanded.

It's not like he wasn't completely expecting the question. But it still made his whole body stiffen.

"The guys' was really crowded, and I had to go," Anthony blurted out. "I drank one of those massive Big Gulps on my way over here. No one was in the girls', so, you know." He shrugged, feeling like a moron.

Rocha made a note on the yellow pad in front of him. Anthony tried not to wince. It wasn't going to be all that hard to check on the crowded-bathroom story, either, he realized. All Rocha would have to do was ask every guy in the place if they'd gone to take a leak around that time.

"I'm sure you've heard a pipe bomb was set off in the girls' bathroom," Rocha said. "Did you notice anything out of the ordinary when you were in there?" Anthony could see Rocha's tongue running around between his top front teeth and his upper lip, like he was trying to get rid of a piece of food or something.

Anthony forced his gaze off Rocha's gross dental hygiene action and went for some eye-to-eye contact, which was supposed to make you look truthful. "I didn't notice anything. Sorry. I wish I had. I would love to help you find whoever did it."

Shut up. Just shut up, Anthony ordered himself. That was way, way too much. Even though he *would* love to find whoever did it and beat them into a bag of squishy pulp. Not for Rae, like he owed her any favors, but for himself.

"Did you see anyone around?" Rocha asked. He made another pass across his teeth with his tongue. "Any other guys decide to use the girls' bathroom because, as you said, the boys' was so full?"

"No," Anthony answered, figuring one-word answers were probably safest.

"Would you mind if I took a look in your back-pack?" Rocha asked. "Just so I have something more solid to tell the police. Then we can all go on to looking for the people who really did this."

Sadistic bastard, Anthony thought. *He's so sure I did it, and he just can't resist really rubbing it in.* Anthony tossed his backpack on the desk. "Go for it," he said. He kept his eyes on Rocha's face, wanting to see the disappointment when he didn't find anything.

But Rocha smiled when he unzipped the

backpack. "Pliers. A dowel. Tissue paper. Superglue. And gunpowder," he said. "All ingredients for a pipe bomb."

Anthony's body went cold. Like all he'd been eating for days was ice cubes. *Somebody set me up,* he thought.

Rae twirled the blue cup in her fingers—
/SO PALE/WHAT ELSE COULD I GET FOR HER /GONNA FIND OUT WHO DID THIS/SHE'S OKAY/
—trying to pay attention to the hack-head girl, who was talking about her feelings. Her feelings about *what,* Rae wasn't exactly sure. Her mind kept wandering to Anthony. And as she twirled the cup—
/SO PALE/WHAT ELSE COULD I GET FOR HER/GONNA FIND OUT WHO DID THIS/SHE'S OKAY/
—with the Anthony-flavored thoughts repeating in her head, getting fuzzier and fuzzier, she kept wishing she'd just kept her mouth shut.

But if she had, who knew what would have happened? Maybe Anthony did set the bomb. Maybe he would have set another one. She set the cup down at her feet. *Maybe, maybe, maybe,* she thought. But maybe he'd just been in the wrong place at the wrong time. Or maybe someone did set him up. Although why the freak thought in her head would be true, she had no idea.

The door to the meeting room opened, and Mr.

Rocha walked in. *Oh God, don't let him want to talk to me again,* Rae thought.

"I just wanted to reassure you that we have already discovered who was responsible for the pipe bomb," Mr. Rocha announced from the doorway. He adjusted his tie, looking sickeningly pleased with himself. "I'm sad to say it was Anthony Fascinelli. He will no longer be a member of your group."

"No way," Jesse burst out. "No way would Anthony do that!"

"Jesse, I know it's hard to—" Ms. Abramson began.

Jesse shoved himself to his feet and took a step toward Mr. Rocha. "What's going to happen to him?"

Rae felt like her heart stopped beating while she waited for the answer.

"The authorities are coming to pick him up," Mr. Rocha answered. "I assume that after the police talk to him, he'll be held in a juvenile detention center until he gets a trial date."

"I'm feeling dizzy," Rae said suddenly. And it was true. Her brain felt like it was spinning inside her skull. "I want to go lie down until my dad gets back."

"Fine," Ms. Abramson said. "Now, Jesse, I want you to—"

Rae didn't hear the rest. She pushed past Mr. Rocha and rushed down the hall. She had to find

Anthony. She had to tell him—she didn't know what she had to tell him. But something.

He's probably in Rocha's office, she thought as she broke into a run. Each step sent pain slamming into the back of her head, but she didn't slow down. There wasn't time.

As soon as she reached the office, she grabbed the doorknob—

/knew Fascinelli was a bad one/

—and jerked on it. Locked. "Anthony, are you in there? It's Rae," she said, keeping her voice low.

There was no answer. But he had to be in there. She glanced down the hall, looking for Rocha. He wasn't coming back. Not yet.

"Anthony. I . . . What I did . . . I didn't know what would happen to you," Rae said.

There was no answer. But she could hear someone moving around in there.

"Could you just say something. Please?" Rae begged.

Silence.

Rae didn't know what else to say. There was probably nothing Anthony would want to hear from her right now. Or ever.

Chapter 6

There will be a day when I will want Rae Voight dead. No, that's not true. I already want Rae Voight dead. But today was not the right day.

The girl has . . . abilities. I know it. I need time to discover exactly what they are. So I must wait. I must watch. I must smile at her as if there is nothing evil developing inside her, as if I don't want to destroy the bitch with my bare hands for what she did to me. When I am finally able to learn her secrets, then it will be time to get rid of her. Not just for revenge—although it really will feel good. But because Rae cannot be trusted. When she becomes confident in the use of her abilities, whatever they are, she will be dangerous to anyone who comes in contact with her. And I will gladly kill her to prevent her from harming an innocent. The way her mother did.

* * *

Anthony slammed open the toilet seat, grabbed the scrub brush, and started scrubbing away. He was the new guy at the detention center, and the new meat always got the crap jobs.

Crap jobs, he thought. *I should be a friggin' comedian.*

"You better not be leaving any brown smears, Fascinelli," one of the guys called from the doorway. "If anyone in our dorm screws up, none of us gets TV privileges tonight."

Anthony gave a grunt and kept on scrubbing. *I should have cleaned the floor first,* he thought. What was wrong with these guys? They weren't five-year-olds. They should have mastered point and shoot by now.

He dunked the brush into the water, then started working on a particularly stubborn stain. It's not like he cared about watching some freakin' TV show. But he knew if he made the other guys miss their tube time, they'd find a way to make him pay. Probably sticking his head in the toilet or something. Then he'd end up throwing some punches, and—it would not be a happy situation.

"Clean enough to eat out of," Anthony muttered as he studied the bowl. He slammed down the seat, sprayed it with the noxious bargain brand cleaner the center used, and started polishing away with a rag, like a good little boy. "You know who should be doing this?" he mumbled. "Rae Voight. I wouldn't have ended up here if it wasn't for her big, fat mouth."

An image of her big, fat mouth flashed into his head. Her lips were actually more juicy than fat, and—Anthony shook his head. He wasn't doing mental porn with Rae. The little snitch.

Anthony shoved down the toilet lid, then sprayed it and that grungy little place behind the lid, where the screws were.

Except Rae's not the one who set me up, Anthony thought. *She's not the one who put the pipe bomb stuff in my backpack.* That just made no sense. But anyway, even though she didn't set him up, if Rae hadn't blabbed to Rocha, no one would have been looking in his backpack, and—

"You have a visitor, Anthony," a voice called. "You can finish up in here when you're done." Anthony backed out of the stall and saw Bible Bob smiling at him. That's what the guys called the man in charge of their dorm—Bible Bob, because he was always quoting the "good book." At least he wasn't one of those jerks who took jobs like this because they got off on taking names and kicking butt.

"You know where the common room is, right?" Bob asked.

"Yeah." Anthony dumped his cleaning stuff in the corner and started washing his hands. "Do you know who it is?"

"Your mom," Bob answered.

Anthony dried his hands on the legs of his jeans. "She alone?"

"Yep. You can have as many visitors as you want—as long as you keep your act together. If there's someone else you want to see—" Bob said.

"There isn't," Anthony interrupted. He strode out of the bathroom past Bob, pasting a good-boy smile on his face, and headed down the hall. *So I don't have to deal with stepdad, the sequel,* he thought. Tom was a decent enough guy. But every once in a while he'd go all father on Anthony. Tom had lived in their house for, like, eight months. He knew nothing about Anthony. Nothing.

When Anthony reached the door to the common room, he hesitated, then pulled in a deep breath and opened the door. His eyes went immediately to his mother. Probably *anyone's* eyes would have gone immediately to his mother. She dressed more like a hooker than a mom most of the time because, as she always said, with what she'd paid for her body, she had to show it off. He bet she'd given several of the guys some new images for their mental porn. *Gee, thanks, Mom.*

"Anthony, over here," his mother cried.

I'm heading right toward you, so obviously I see you, he thought. But that was another thing about his mom. She was loud. He took one more step, and she was out of her chair and coming toward him, screeching his name. Then she had him wrapped in a tight, hard hug, the smell of her floral perfume almost choking him.

Anthony knew that the other guys in the room had to be looking, but he didn't let his mother go. For one long moment he closed his eyes and just held on, held on until she finally stepped away.

"Oh, baby, what were you thinking?" his mother asked.

Of course she just assumes I did it, Anthony thought. He opened his mouth to protest, then snapped it shut. He didn't want to have this little talk in the middle of the room. He stalked over to the table in the corner and sat down. At least it was empty, although there were people at the two tables surrounding it.

His mother took her time sliding onto the bench across from him. "What were you thinking?" she repeated, her voice twice as loud as anyone else's in the room. Anthony knew there was no point in trying to get her to keep it down. If he said something, the next few words would come out softer, then the volume would automatically go back up. It's like she couldn't help herself.

"You realize they called me at work. I had to tell my boss why I was leaving early," his mother continued. "Do you know how that made me feel?"

"I didn't do it," Anthony muttered. "And thanks for asking."

"Anthony, they found the stuff in your backpack." Tears welled up in his mother's eyes.

Oh, great. Just perfect, he thought. His mother cried even louder than she talked. In another few seconds she'd be giving everyone in the place a real show.

"Somebody set me up," Anthony told her.

"It's these boys you hang around with. If you had nice boys as friends, things like this wouldn't happen," his mother answered. The tears were hanging off her eyelashes now. "I tried to . . . to help you. Remember? I made . . . those parties? And . . . and . . ."

And we're off, Anthony thought as his mother started in with the big, gulping sobs. Maybe it would have been better if Tom had come with her. He'd at least have tried to keep her somewhat in line, even though he'd have been totally pissed at Anthony.

His mother started rooting through her purse, probably looking for Kleenex, her crying so loud, it was practically echoing. Anthony focused his eyes on a crack in the linoleum floor. He couldn't look at her right now.

Just let her go, he told himself. There was no point in trying to say anything. When she got on a crying jag, it was like she went deaf or something. She wouldn't be able to listen to him until she was finished with her little fit.

"I don't know what I'm supposed to do. Tell me what I'm supposed to do," she said, snuffling and sniffling. "I can't follow you around all day, making sure that you don't get into trouble. I would if I could. But I have to work. You know that."

Anthony heard a snicker. He gripped the edge of the bench with both hands. If he didn't, he'd have to punch someone.

Her crying got a little quieter. She was winding down. "There's nothing you're supposed to do," Anthony told her. "You do everything a mother's supposed to do."

He heard another snicker, but he ignored it. "Look, just don't worry," he continued. "At my trial everything will get straightened out. Everything will be fine." Because it's not like there was any *evidence* against him or anything. Just a backpack full of pipe bomb crap and an eyewitness who could place him in the bathroom.

"But what if—" his mother began.

Anthony couldn't let her get started again. He leaned across the table and kissed her cheek. "It won't," he answered. "Now, you should go. It's almost time for Carl to take his antibiotics again. Tom won't remember."

His mother stood up, patted her hair, then pulled out a lipstick and added a fresh coat. "I'll come and see you tomorrow."

"Don't ask for more time off work, okay?" Anthony said. "I'm all right." He saw that her eyes were refilling with tears. He stood up fast, kissed her again, then hurried out of the room.

A few seconds later he heard footsteps in the hall behind him.

"Fascinelli's mom is hot," a voice said.

Anthony didn't turn around.

"Yeah, did you see her boobs? She's got to be a double D," another voice answered. "Started giving me a stiffy."

Anthony didn't turn around. Getting in a fight on his first day in this place would be a total Bluebird move.

"What about you, Anthony?" the first voice called. "When you gave your mommy those kisses, did it get you excited?"

If we weren't in here, you guys would already be bleeding, Anthony thought. But they were in here.

And who knew how long Anthony would have to stay?

Why couldn't Rae just have given him a freakin' break?

Rae started slowly toward the cafeteria. She wasn't ready for another round of Who Wants to Be Sickeningly Nice to Rae? Being nice should be a good thing, she guessed. But her friends were sooo nice, it made Rae feel like a freak. Or like a charity project. Dori Hernandez was the worst. She'd stare at Rae with these big, sympathetic eyes—while practically sitting on Marcus's lap.

When she reached the double doors, she pushed through them—

*I talked to me a lot/*my perfect brother wouldn't/*will Rae go off again if/*

—without hesitation. *Attitude,* she reminded herself for the billionth time. She strode over to the food line and grabbed a tray—

/didn't have to act like I was/*iced tea/*

—then took a bean burrito even though she didn't feel hungry. *You're eating it all,* she told herself. She hadn't eaten anything last night or this morning. And she was *not* going to go anorexic. She had enough problems. She took a carton of milk, paid, and got change, a burst of static filling her head. Way underneath Rae thought there were words, but she couldn't make them out. She'd gotten a bunch of the little static blasts since she was hospitalized. Just another little variation on her "specialness."

Rae turned toward her usual table. Lea was laughing at something Vincent had just said. *If I go over there, she'll stop laughing,* Rae thought. *She'll go into her overprotective mode—making sure I have napkins, making sure I got enough food, making sure that everyone is being nice to me, which of course everyone will be, at least to my face.*

Still, she had to keep trying, right? One of these days her friends would have to go back to normal around her. She took a deep breath and headed toward them.

"So it's okay if we don't invite Rae, right?" she heard Jackie's familiar voice say just as she neared the table. She stopped, her heart slamming against her chest. Invite Rae where?

Rae turned her back to them and rested her tray down on an empty table, holding her breath as she listened.

"It's better for her," she heard Lea answer, a note of defensiveness in her voice. "I don't think she'd really be up for a party yet."

"That's what I figured," Jackie said quickly. "So Dori, you and Marcus can—"

Rae jammed the carton of milk and the burrito into

her backpack, letting the not-her thoughts flow through her mind as she spun back around and speed walked toward the exit. No food was supposed to be taken out of the cafeteria, but screw that. If she had to sit at the table with her quote-unquote friends, she wouldn't be able to swallow a bite. She hurried back out the doors—

/*Carrie White*/door—puerta/

—and started down the hall, blinking rapidly. It was one thing when they were all treating her like some little kid that practically needed to be spoon-fed. At least she still felt like they cared. But to hear them sitting there coming up with excuses to keep her out of their social life—that was too much.

Maybe she could eat in the art room. She could hang out there, do some work on her painting. Rae jerked to a stop. *Yeah, working on that painting would really help your appetite,* she thought.

She'd just started another one of those paintings where her hand did what it wanted. Big mistake. She'd ended up with the beginnings of a face that she absolutely knew would become Anthony Fascinelli. Anthony Fascinelli, looking at her like he wanted her dead.

God, how much did she wish she hadn't said any-thing to Mr. Rocha yesterday? All she could think about now was those not-her thoughts that felt like

Anthony, the thoughts that kept trying to convince her that he was innocent. *If he is or if he isn't, there's nothing you can do about it now,* she told herself.

A couple of girls from her English class passed her, giving her semiweird looks. *Could it be because I'm standing in the middle of the hall like I have no idea where I should go?* she asked herself. Rae headed toward the stairwell. She could eat there without anyone looking at her or being nice. No, not nice. *Fake* nice.

Pretty pathetic, she thought as she opened the door.

/will she be here?/

She pulled a notebook out of her backpack, letting the not-her thoughts roll on by, and put it on the top step so she'd have something to sit on. *I'm not going to walk around all day with a dirty butt,* she thought. *People are staring enough as it is.* Before she could even retrieve her burrito, the door swung open behind her.

Oh, great. Probably a couple looking to make out. *Please don't let it be Dori and Marcus.* She glanced over her shoulder and saw Jeff Brunner standing there.

"Hey," he said, looking a little embarrassed. "I saw you come in here and . . ." He let the sentence trail off.

Rae raised an eyebrow. "You just *happened* to see me come in here?"

"I was looking for you in the cafeteria," Jeff confessed, one of his adorable blushes coloring his face. Rae bet he hated being a blusher. "I saw you leave," he continued. "Then I sort of followed you, and that's when I happened to see you come in here."

Oh my God Is he actually interested *in me?* Rae searched his face, looking for any hint that he was doing his good deed for the day or getting his jollies by hanging out with the school nut job. But his smile was just a nice, normal, slightly shy smile. And he had no problem with meeting her eyes; well, except for when he did one of those fast guy eye drops and checked out her body.

Rae allowed herself a quick body scan on Jeff. He was tall and lean, with a swimmer kind of build versus the football-player type. Nice.

"So, um, what do you think of Sanderson so far?" Rae asked. She got her foil-wrapped burrito out of her backpack and unwrapped it, ignoring the blurry thought.

"I'm liking it more all the time," he answered, looking right at her.

Rae laughed in his face. His blush got a little deeper, but he laughed, too. "Smooth, huh?" he asked.

"Oh, yeah, real smooth," she answered. He was flirting with her. And she was actually kind of flirting back. How bizarre was that? Rae Voight was actually having a basically normal encounter at Sanderson Prep. Yeah, it was in the stairwell, but still. She took a bite of her burrito, suddenly starving. "Aren't you going to eat?"

"Eat. Right," Jeff said. He sat down next to her and pulled a sandwich and a bag of pork rinds out of his backpack. "Want some?" He shook the pork rinds in her direction.

"I'm a vegetarian," Rae answered, wrinkling her nose.

Jeff hurled the pork rinds down the stairs. "So am I. Those things disgust me."

Rae actually giggled. How long had it been since she'd done that? She was surprised she hadn't forgotten how.

"Some sicko put them in my backpack," Jeff told her. "You believe me, right?"

"Of course I believe you," Rae answered with mock sincerity.

She couldn't help thinking of Anthony. Who could have put the pipe bomb stuff in his backpack? Everyone had been talking about it after the meeting yesterday. She pushed the thought away. For once she had the chance to be . . . the girl she used to be. The girl who could flirt, knowing that the guy would like it.

"Really," Jeff insisted. "I never eat those things."

"You better not," Rae teased. "I could never sit this close to a guy with pork-rind breath."

Jeff moved a little closer, just the tiniest bit, but close enough that Rae could feel the heat of his body. "How do you feel about peanut butter?" he asked, holding up his sandwich.

"I'm totally for it," Rae answered.

He started to take a bite. "Strawberry jelly?"

"The best," Rae said. "You have my permission and my approval to eat it."

Jeff took a bite, then held the sandwich up to Rae's lips. She took a bite, too.

Let me spend the rest of my life right here, she thought. *Right here with this one moment stretching out forever. That's all I want. It wouldn't take one other thing to make me happy if I could keep on feeling normal. Just normal.*

Chapter 7

Rae headed across her front lawn, eager to get inside the house. She had about two hours of total alone time. No school. No group. No Dad. And no housekeeper, thank God. Her dad had actually wanted to hire someone as a live-in housekeeper, aka baby-sitter, when Rae got out of the hospital, but she'd managed to convince him she could be trusted in the house by herself for the, like, two or three minutes a day when she was there without him. And they still had Alice Shaffer come in twice a week to clean and freeze some meals for them.

She pulled out her key—

I just let me!

—and unlocked the door, then grabbed the knob. She gasped when her fingers touched it—

/that bitch, Rae/

—and she jerked them away. The thought had been like a scream in her mind, so full of hate that it made her nerves sizzle. It hadn't *felt* like anyone familiar, the way some of the thoughts had started to. But that almost made it worse. It was like there was a stranger in her head who wanted to hurt her.

Just go get in the tub with some of that Baby Bee milk bath stuff, put your plastic cushion under your head, and veg until you're a prune, Rae told herself. *You can even get in some fantasizing about that guy Jeff. He'll make good mind candy.* She forced herself to open the door—

/that bitch, Rae/

—then stepped inside and closed it behind her.

/if I get caught/

Rae's heart gave a kick in her chest and started beating double time. That thought had been so full of anxiety that it had affected her body—even though she knew the thought wasn't really her own. *You've got to let them rush through,* she instructed herself. *They're mind Muzak, nothing more. Annoying, but that's all.*

Her little self-lecture didn't slow down her heart. She started for the kitchen to make herself some hot chocolate to drink in the tub. Somehow warm water outside and warm chocolate inside really got her into the calm zone, despite the caffeine thing.

Why is the hall light on? she thought. Her dad had a fit about anyone wasting electricity, so Rae was in the habit of turning off the lights when she left the house. And he never forgot. She veered over and flicked off the switch.

/Rae'll be sorry/

God, it was the same, the same *flavor* as the other not her thoughts she'd gotten—the ones off the door. That person who hated her. Even with the static she could tell that. Who could hate her so much?

"Not a who. Muzak," she whispered. "That's all." But the little hairs on her arms were standing up. So were the ones on the back of her neck. Rae glanced behind her. No one was there. But she didn't feel alone. She could swear there was someone in the house with her. A shiver slithered through her, and she wrapped her arms around herself. But it didn't make her feel any warmer.

Okay, forget the bath, she thought. *This is way beyond bath comfort. Call Yana. Invite her over. She already knows you're part squirrel. She won't get weirded out if you confess that you want company because you're giving yourself the creeps.* Rae rushed down the hall to her bedroom and yanked open the door.

/teach her/

"No," she whispered. "I don't—why?" Her brain felt like it was hardly functioning. She pulled in a deep breath and tried to take in what she was seeing.

Her comforter had been shredded. Clumps of the cotton batting were lying all over the floor, along with pieces of glass that Rae recognized as the remnants of her perfume bottles. Each breath burned Rae's throat and lungs, and it didn't feel like she was getting oxygen, just a mix of citrus and musk and flowers.

Don't just stand there. Run! she told herself. But she couldn't stop staring around the room. The canvas of her newest painting had been slashed. Rufus, her very first stuffed animal, had been ripped almost in two. Rae knelt down, picked up the worn bunny—

/teach her/

—and cradled it in her arms. Was this some kind of hallucination? Was she becoming even more psycho? What if she called Yana and Yana said the room looked perfectly ordinary? Rae squeezed Rufus tighter.

/teach her/

She walked over to her dresser, the glass crunching under her feet, then leaned down and stared into her mirror, as if looking at herself would tell her whether she was becoming like her mother. More like her mother. Becoming totally, irretrievably insane.

Her blue eyes looked scared, but not crazy. *As if a crazy person would be able to make that call,* she thought. She started to straighten up, then froze. There were words reflected in the mirror. Words that had been painted on the wall behind her.

Slowly Rae turned around and read the message that had been left for her: *Keep your big mouth shut.* She walked over and ran her fingers over the words. They were still wet.

This would be a very good time to get out of here. A very, very good time. She took one step toward the door, then froze again. She'd heard something. A tiny sound coming from the bathroom.

Whoever had done this to her was still in the house.

Anthony locked his eyes on the tube, not that he cared which of the idiots on *Ricki Lake* had slept with which of the other idiots. It's just that he wanted to blend, and shutting up and watching TV was the easiest way to do it.

"Did you hear what happened to McGlynn?" one of the guys on the couch asked. Anthony knew the guy wasn't talking to him, so he didn't even glance over. This wasn't a place where you just joined in a conversation.

"What?" some other guy asked.

"Got sent to Ashton," the first guy answered.

Anthony tried to actually pay attention to the *Ricki* freaks. The last thing he wanted to listen to was a bunch of crap about Ashton. If things went bad at his trial, he'd be at the youth prison soon enough, and then he'd see it all for himself.

"Fascinelli, your head is in the way," said Paul, a guy from Anthony's dorm. Anthony slid over a foot and crossed his legs, trying to get comfortable again on the floor's thin carpet.

"It's still in the way," Paul said.

Anthony didn't move. Clearly Paul was making a little power play. If Anthony moved again, he knew Paul would keep pushing him, trying to figure out exactly how much Anthony would take. He figured it was better to deal with Paul now instead of letting it escalate.

"Are you deaf?" Paul asked. He gave Anthony a kick in the back. Not too hard, but hard enough.

Anthony shot a glance over at Bible Bob. He was in the middle of an earnest conversation with one of the younger kids. Anthony turned back to the TV, then he reached over and grabbed Paul by the ankle. He gave a hard jerk, and Paul came out of the chair and landed on his butt on the floor. "Now can you see?"

A couple of guys laughed. Anthony didn't. He wasn't trying to score points. He was just trying to make it through his stretch here without getting the crap beat out of him. And if he had to be a badass to do it, so be it.

Some of the tension drained out of his body as he realized that Paul wasn't going to try taking things to the next level. At least not this time.

"If you tried that at Ashton, you'd be missing a limb right about now," one of the guys on the couch commented.

"I'm not going to Ashton," Anthony muttered.

I wouldn't be able to survive it if I did, he thought. *I'd freakin' die if I ended up there.*

If. Yeah, right. Big *if.* The police would show all the stuff Rocha found in Anthony's backpack. Rae would say she saw him *inside* the girls' bathroom. There was no *if* in this scenario. He was going down.

Should she try to leave? Just run for it? Rae shifted her weight from foot to foot. What if she wasn't fast enough? What if whoever was in the bathroom caught her? Maybe she should just hide in the closet or something. Wait him out.

She hesitated. Neither solution felt right. *You have to do* something, she ordered herself. Then she heard the bathroom door swing open. If she ran, he would see her. If she darted to the closet, he would hear her.

Footsteps started down the hall toward her room.

A figure started past the open door. Rae didn't think. She just let out a howl that was half terror and half fury and hurled herself at the guy. He hit the ground with a thud, and she heard his breath come out with a wheeze.

"Who are you?" she demanded, voice shaking. Then she realized the guy was smaller than she thought at first, just about her size. Rae roughly flipped him over onto his back. She recognized his face immediately. It took a second longer to come up with his name. "Jesse," she cried. "Jesse Beven, from group. You did this? Why would you do this?"

Jesse started to struggle to his knees, but Rae shoved him back down. His face was so white that she could see every freckle. *He's as scared as I was,* she thought. "Answer me," she barked.

"I don't have to tell you anything." He jerked his body to the left and managed to scramble up before Rae could grab him again. He took off down the hall.

"Hey, Mensa boy, I know your name," Rae called after him as she shoved herself to her feet. He stopped. "Ms. Abramson knows where you live and your phone number," she continued. "By the time you get home, the police will be waiting for you."

Jesse turned around. "Fine. Get me sent to the detention center with Anthony. I'd rather be there."

"So that's what your little painting on my wall

was about. Anthony," Rae said. She let Rufus fall to the ground.

"Duh," Jesse muttered. He jerked up his chin, and his red hair fell away from his face.

God, he was a baby. Barely thirteen.

"Look, my dad will be home in a few hours. Clean up my room before he gets here, and I might be able to forget this ever happened," Rae told him. "You can pay me back for the stuff you trashed. A little every week," she added.

Jesse stared at her for a long moment. Then he walked over, picked up Rufus from the ground, and handed him to her. He stepped past her into her room without a word. Rae followed him. She put Rufus on her bed, feeling overwhelmed by the amount of damage Jesse had managed to do. "I'll get some garbage bags," she said, hurrying to the kitchen without waiting for an answer.

She opened the polished doorknob of the little supply cupboard, a closet she and her dad rarely bothered going into since most of their cleaning involved paper towels and water, and pulled out a box of the jumbo lawn trash bags—

/need to pick up candles/

—then rushed back to her room. She didn't want to leave Jesse alone too long in case he thought about bolting again. Not something she wanted to have to deal with.

"Here." She lobbed the box of trash bags at Jesse, who was crouched on the floor, gathering up pieces of comforter stuffing.

He gave a grunt that she decided to take as a thank-you.

Might as well help, she thought. She grabbed some turpentine and some rags from a box in her closet, letting the not-her thoughts—although these were of the variety that felt *more* like her—buzz on through her brain, then started working on getting the paint off the wall. Her father would freak if he saw it. Forget about a live-in housekeeper; he'd probably hire an armed guard.

They worked in silence, without looking at each other. "Can I open a window?" Jesse finally asked.

"Yeah. It reeks in here," Rae answered. "And by the way, you're going to have to cough up some major bucks for the perfume."

"I will. It was stupid. It's just—you don't know Anthony," Jesse blurted out. "I do. He would never have set off that pipe bomb. There's no way."

He was saying what Rae had been thinking. Make that what she'd been hoping. *Are we both delusional?* Rae wondered. She turned to face him. "How long have you known Anthony?"

"Couple of years," Jesse answered. "And I know he wouldn't set off a pipe bomb. When Anthony gets pissed, he just starts throwing punches. He doesn't stop and plan, like you'd have to do to set a bomb."

"So you're saying he's violent. But too hot tempered to take the time to plant a bomb?" Rae asked sarcastically, even though a part of her, a big part of her, wanted to believe Anthony was innocent. She just didn't want to be an idiot about it.

"Forget it," Jesse mumbled. "You don't want to hear it." He tied one of the garbage bags closed with a tight knot.

Rae crossed the room and sat down next to him. She opened a fresh garbage bag and started picking up pieces of her perfume bottles, fragments of thoughts popping up in her head every few shards. "I do want to hear it," she finally said. "I just don't want to be played."

"I'm not playing you," Jesse answered as he gathered some pieces of glass in one cupped hand. "Anthony gets in fights when people piss him off." He dumped the glass into the bag. "Like when this guy at the 7-Eleven was busting on me, Anthony broke his nose. Blood geyser."

Jesse sounded way too impressed. Rae shook her head.

"He totally backed me up, with no questions. That's what you'd get if you knew him. You should see the garbage he does for his little brothers and sister. He even wore a Backstreet Boys T-shirt one day so he wouldn't hurt his little sister's feelings."

So that was why he'd worn the stupid shirt. She picked up another piece of glass, and a tiny sliver jammed itself into her finger. She carefully began prying it out with one fingernail, trying not to get all gooey over the picture of Anthony being that sweet to his little sister.

"So if Anthony didn't do it, who did?" Rae asked, pulling the glass sliver free. She sucked lightly on the cut, which was barely bleeding—just a couple of drops. She was curious to see if Jesse had any theories. She'd love some hard info instead of her thoughts and feelings, which she'd be crazy—literally—to trust.

Jesse shrugged. "I just know it wasn't Anthony," he answered, without a hint of doubt or deceit in his voice.

"The stuff was in his backpack," Rae reminded him.

"Then somebody set him up," Jesse shot back.

Gonna find out who did this. She remembered how good it had made her feel when she'd held that blue cup and heard that thought the first time. That Anthony-flavored thought. It had made her feel kind of warm inside. Safe. Like someone was looking out for her. And from what Jesse said, Anthony *was* the kind of guy who did that—looked out for people.

You can't start believing your Looney Tunes thoughts, she reminded herself. But she felt almost positive that Jesse was telling her the truth. And her own instincts, or whatever you wanted to call them, agreed.

"Maybe you're right," Rae said softly.

"What?" Jesse exclaimed.

"I said, maybe you're right about Anthony," Rae told him. "Now, keep cleaning."

Chapter 8

"Rae. Over here!" Yana called. Rae smiled as she spotted Yana in the school parking lot, leaning against her beat-up sunshine yellow VW Bug.

"Nice pants," Rae said as she hurried over.

"Just the pants? What, you don't like the shirt?" Yana asked. She adjusted the collar of her turquoise bowling shirt. Rae noticed that the name Betty was embroidered over the pocket.

"No, I like. But python pants, high-heel boots, and bowling shirt." Rae shook her head. "One of these things is not like the other."

"That's me. Full of surprises," Yana answered. "And the pants are faux, by the way. No actual snakes died to make me a fashion superstar." She opened the car door and slid behind the wheel. Rae took the shot-gun seat, some of her own special Muzak playing in her head.

"Thanks for taking me," Rae said. "I could have bused it, but—"

"Oh, shut up," Yana interrupted. "We're friends, remember?"

Rae could feel her smile widening into something that was probably ridiculous looking. The casual way that Yana used the word *friend*—it made her feel all toasty inside. Which was pathetic but true.

Rae's cell phone rang, and she pulled it out of her purse and answered it, trying not to let the not-her thoughts popping up in her head distract her.

"Hi, Rae. It's Ms. Abramson. Your dad gave me this number. I hope that's okay with you," she said.

"Yeah. Fine," Rae answered, although she wished he hadn't. It was hard to feel normal when your group therapy leader could call you anywhere, anytime.

"I just wanted to let you know we'll miss you in group this afternoon," Ms. Abramson continued.

"Um, thanks," Rae said, not adding that she wouldn't miss Ms. Abramson or anyone else. Not having to sit around and emote with the other sickos was the one bonus of having to go to the police station and give a statement. Plus she got to hang with Yana.

"I know it's probably a little scary for you to talk to

the police. But all you have to do is tell them what you saw," Ms. Abramson said, her voice filled with concern. "Call me afterward if you want to talk things through."

"Okay. I will. I have to go, but thanks." Rae hung up without waiting for Ms. Abramson to say good-bye, then stuck her phone back in her purse.

"Nice cell," Yana commented.

"Nice tracking device," Rae corrected her. "It was a present from my dad. I think he thinks if he can be in touch with me at any moment that somehow I won't have another psycho fit."

Yana shot Rae an irritated look, her green eyes narrowed, as she pulled to a stop in front of a red light. "Okay. Here's the deal. The next time you use the word *psycho* or *freak* about yourself, I'm going to slap you. And I'm talking hard," Yana warned.

"What about if I just say"—Rae leaned toward Yana and lowered her voice to a whisper—"that I'm not quite my old self." She returned her voice to a normal level. "I heard someone saying that about me when I was in the bathroom today. Doesn't anyone bother to check under the stall doors anymore?"

"Clearly whoever said that has no life," Yana answered. "If they did, they wouldn't be hanging around in the bathroom, talking about *you*." She gunned her engine at the Jag next to her. The guy behind the wheel grinned.

"Yana, that guy has to be, like, thirty," Rae protested.

"But damn cute," Yana answered as the light changed and they started across the intersection. "So what's the scoopage on you guywise?"

Thank God Yana volunteered to drive me, Rae thought. If she'd been on the bus, she'd be thinking about Anthony nonstop. Actually, she still sort of was, with an underlayer of her brain. But at least part of her attention was on the conversation with Yana. Her friend. Rae couldn't stop the dopey smile from appearing again.

"From the look on your face, I'd say guywise you're doing okay," Yana teased.

"Oh, sure. Except for the little fact that my old boyfriend dumped me. Not that he actually ever bothered to say so. He just appeared the first day of school with this girl Dori Hernandez surgically attached to him," Rae answered, the words coming out bitter. Big surprise.

"Yowch," Yana said with a grimace.

"Yeah. But I met this other guy. Jeff," Rae added quickly, not wanting to seem like a total loser. "We've only hung out a few times. Just at lunch, you know. But—"

"But you looove him," Yana said. She made a right turn so fast, Rae's seat belt cut into her side.

"He has his good points," Rae admitted. "One of the big ones is that he's new. So even though he heard about me losing it last year, he didn't actually witness my psy—"

Yana held up one hand. "I'm warning you."

"He doesn't act all weird around me," Rae amended, avoiding the slap.

"So give me the stats," Yana said.

"Um, okay. Tall. Light brown hair. Nice hands, you know?" Rae began.

"Boring. What about his butt?" Yana asked.

"That's also nice," Rae answered. *Last year this is exactly the kind of conversation I'd have been having with Lea,* Rae realized.

"We're almost there. Are you starting to get worried about talking to the cops?" Yana asked. "It's not going to be a big deal. You say what happened. They write it down. Badda-bing. Badda-boom. It's over."

"Except for Anthony," Rae said.

"Not your problem," Yana answered.

Yeah, but if I'd kept my mouth shut, Anthony'd be out shooting hoops or whatever right now, Rae thought. *Which makes it my problem in a way.*

Yana pulled the Bug into the parking lot of the police station and found a parking place right in front of the building. "And anyway," she continued. "It's not like what you have to say matters that much. They found all that bomb junk in his backpack, right?"

"Right," Rae replied. "Right," she repeated.

But that was just circumstantial evidence. It didn't prove anything. It didn't make the accusations against Anthony true. What felt true was Jesse's belief that Anthony wasn't capable of the kind of cruelty it would take to set off the bomb. What felt true was Rae's own belief—based on pretty much nothing— that Anthony was innocent.

"I'll be waiting for you when you're done," Yana told her. "We'll get ice cream."

Rae nodded. "Thanks again, Ya—"

"Didn't I tell you to shut up about it?" Yana interrupted. She gave Rae's shoulder a shove.

"Okay, okay. I'm going. See you in a little while. At least I hope it won't take long." Rae climbed out of the car and slammed the door.

/need better ID/

Then she headed up to the glass front door and pushed it open—

/why did he/can't be here again/so wasted/

—and headed over to the cop at the front desk. "I'm Rae Voight. I have an appointment with Detective Sullivan."

The cop nodded, adjusting the clump of hair he'd combed over his bald spot. He picked up the phone, hit a couple of numbers. "The girl is here," he said.

Thanks for remembering my name, Rae thought.

"She'll be right out," he told Rae. "You can sit over there." The cop jerked his head toward a long wooden bench against the wall behind her. Rae obediently walked over and plopped down. Her stomach was already twisting itself into an extreme pretzel, and she hadn't even seen the detective yet.

Rae took her brush out of her purse—

/need a trim/**Anthony wouldn't**/

—and began pulling it through her hair. She was getting better and better at picking up on the flavors of the not her thoughts. Weirdly, that first not-her one actually felt like her. But not. Like it was a thought of hers but not the thought she was actually having at that moment. Whatever that was supposed to mean.

And the other one, it had given her a Jesse vibe. The mix of anger and fear and frustration just felt like him somehow. The kid was going nuts thinking that Anthony might get sent away. Talking to Jesse while they cleaned had given Rae the idea that Anthony was pretty much Jesse's surrogate big brother. It had also given her the idea that Jesse needed one.

How am I even going to look at Jesse in group if I help nail Anthony? Rae thought. Before she could come up with an answer, a forty-something woman strode toward her, looking much more glam than Rae expected, with an ash blond bob and perfectly manicured nails. "Rae? I'm Laura Sullivan," she said, giving Rae's hand a quick, firm shake. "Come on back."

Detective Sullivan led Rae through a maze of desks and into a grungy office. Clearly she'd tried to make it a little nicer with some potted plants and a Picasso print on the wall—one with a woman looking in a mirror. *A gutsy choice, considering how many guys she worked with,* Rae thought. But nothing Ms. Sullivan had done could compensate for the ugly metal desk, the beat-up chairs, the stained carpet, and the worst shade of green paint Rae'd ever seen. "We'll make this short," Ms. Sullivan said. "I'm sure that you have other things you'd rather be doing."

"Pretty much anything," Rae admitted, sitting in the chair voted the most likely not to collapse.

"Just tell me what you saw." Ms. Sullivan positioned her hands on her computer keyboard.

Easy for you to say, Rae thought. If she told what she saw, she'd ruin Anthony's life.

Ms. Sullivan tapped her fingers on the keys impatiently. Rae took the hint. "Okay. Well. I stopped off in the ladies' room. I just wanted to check my makeup," she began. "I stepped toward the mirror. And then I was on the floor. I didn't even realize a bomb had gone off until they told me."

Gotta do something, she thought. *Gotta do something right now to stop this thing. But what?*

"I hit my head," Rae added quickly. "Things got a little fuzzy."

Now, that just might get you—you and Anthony—out of this freakin' mess, Rae told herself. *You hit your head. You don't remember too well what happened. Yeah.*

"I bet," Detective Sullivan said as she typed. "Then what happened?"

Rae brushed her hair off her face. "Then I . . . I was sort of dizzy. There were white dots in front of my eyes and everything, you know?" Ms. Sullivan nodded. "I grabbed the sink and pulled myself up. . . ."

Rae suddenly pictured herself blurting out what really happened next.

And that's when I got one of my not-me thoughts. One that said Anthony could have been set up. Oh, and by the way, I also got a thought saying somebody wanted to kill me. That helps, right? You know not to bother with Anthony. And you know the real bomb setter is someone who would like me dead. Oh, and probably I should tell you that I was recently released from a mental hospital. But that has nothing to do with the thoughts. They were real. That's how I know Anthony is innocent. Well, that, and that when I touched this blue cup, I could tell he was really worried about me, that he really cared. And that makes him a good person. And a good person wouldn't set off a pipe bomb.

So you can call the juvenile detention center right now and tell them there's been a mistake.

"You pulled yourself up and then . . . ?" Ms. Sullivan prompted.

"It's kind of fuzzy," Rae said. "I know that someone helped me down to the nurse's office."

"Let's go back to when you first went into the bathroom," Ms. Sullivan said. "Did you notice anything unusual? See anyone?"

You know I did, Rae thought. *You already heard everything from Rocha.* "Like I said, it's blurry," Rae answered. She shifted in her chair, unable to find a comfortable position.

"It's blurry even before the bomb went off?" Ms. Sullivan asked.

Oh God. I'm such a moron. My whole brilliant fuzzy-thinking story doesn't make any sense. Because I saw Anthony in the bathroom before the bomb went off. Which, naturally, was before I hit my head.

"It's weird," Rae answered slowly, hoping for inspiration. "When I think about going to Oakvale that day, it's all a little, you know, fuzzy. I *did* hit my head pretty hard. It was bleeding in back and *everything.*" *And clearly inspiration did not come,* she thought.

Ms. Sullivan looked up from her computer screen and studied Rae's face. Rae felt like she had the

144

words *big, fat liar* written in lipstick on her forehead.

"Do you remember telling Mr. Rocha what happened?" Ms. Sullivan asked.

"Sort of," Rae admitted.

"You told him that someone was in the bathroom when you went in. Do you remember that?" Ms. Sullivan pressed, her eyes alert, the kind of eyes that noticed everything.

This is hopeless, Rae thought. *Rocha can testify to what I said. I'm just looking suspicious by all this "fuzzy" bull. And it's not helping Anthony, either.*

"Yeah. I remember," Rae answered.

"And who was it you saw?" Ms. Sullivan asked.

Rae met Ms. Sullivan's gaze straight on. Then she said the only thing she could say.

"It was Anthony Fascinelli."

Anthony headed to the common room. He prayed his mother would be wearing something that wouldn't get too much attention from the guys. He pushed open the door—and saw Jesse sitting at the table in the back corner. But he wasn't alone—Rae was sitting next to him.

No way. He had to take a lot of crap in this place. But he did not have to take this. Anthony strode over to the table and leaned down until he could look Rae directly in the eye. "Get out of here," he ordered. "Right now."

"She wants to help," Jesse said.

"Bull," Anthony shot back without taking his eyes off Rae, careful to keep his voice low enough so that the counselor supervising the room wouldn't hear. "I wouldn't be here if it wasn't for her."

"Sit down, Mr. Fascinelli," the counselor called from across the room. Anthony sat, still locking eyes with Rae. Her gaze finally skittered away from his, and he felt a surge of satisfaction.

"That's not totally true, you know," Rae protested, her eyes lowered and her voice all whiny. "They found the stuff in your backpack, so—"

"They wouldn't have been looking in my backpack if you hadn't opened your fat mouth," Anthony shot back.

Rae's chin jerked up. "What were you doing in the girls' bathroom in the first place? And forget that the-guys'-was-flooded fairy tale." Her voice wasn't whiny now. It was sharp, accusing. And this time she was the one getting in *his* face, going practically nose to nose with him, blue eyes bright with anger. Like *she* had anything to be angry about.

"I can't believe you're coming in here asking me questions," Anthony said. He shot a glance at Jesse. "I hope this wasn't your idea."

"It wasn't," Rae answered. "Look, let's back up, okay?" She reached out and touched his wrist for a fraction of a second, and he felt the heat of her fingers

146

down to the bone. "I didn't come here—" She hesitated, started again. "I came here because I don't think you set off the bomb. And I don't want to be part of putting you into Ashton."

Ashton. The word was like a bullet to the gut.

"There's nothing either of you can do about it." He gave Rae a pointed look. "Unless you plan on lying to the cops."

"I already gave them my testimony," Rae admitted. She gave his wrist another one of those fast finger brushes. "I'd already told Rocha everything. I thought it would make things worse if I changed my story. I'm sorry."

"So you're here so I can say, 'Oh, that's okay. I know you feel bad, but it's not your fault.' Is that it?" Anthony's hands curled into fists. He willed himself to make them relax.

"That's not why we came. We're going to figure out who did do it," Jesse said eagerly.

"What are you? The friggin' Hardy Boys?" Anthony asked. He felt a twinge of guilt when he saw the hurt expression on Jesse's face. But really, what were they thinking?

"We're what you have," Rae said quietly. "And it's not like anything we do is going to make things any worse." Jesse didn't say anything. He wouldn't even look Anthony in the face.

Anthony scrubbed his face with his fingers. "You're right," he admitted. "So, what's the plan? Is there a plan?"

"Not yet," Rae said. "We thought if you could just tell us . . . something, we'd, uh, try and dig up some evidence."

Her face turned pink all the way to the roots of her hair, like she was embarrassed to be saying that crap. And she should be. This was freakin' hopeless.

"Why *were* you in the girls' bathroom?" Jesse asked, shoulders hunched like he was afraid to say the words. "They're definitely going to ask you that at your hearing."

"The guy I buy weed from said he left some for me in there," Anthony said. He did a check on the counselor. The guy was still too far away to hear, hovering by a table where a girlfriend had brought her boyfriend some brownies, clearly hoping for a handout.

"In the girls' bathroom?" Rae asked.

"The guy's a moron," Anthony answered. "But even for Nunan this was a new low."

"So it's not the usual place for a pickup," Jesse said. And he actually pulled a little notebook and a pencil out of his pocket.

Anthony shook his head. "I usually just go over to the 7-Eleven and get it from him."

"So, okay," Rae said. "I'm no Nancy Drew, but I say the first thing we do is talk to this Nunan guy. See why he chose the girls' bathroom. And find out if he saw anything when he made the drop." She glanced at Jesse, and he gave a little nod, then started scribbling away. They were quite a pair.

"Couldn't hurt, I guess," Anthony said. He locked his hands behind his head and leaned back, trying to crack his spine. It felt like it was made of cement or something.

"Don't sound so grateful," Rae told him, a little irritation creeping into her voice.

"Is that why you're here? You want gratitude?" Anthony demanded.

"No," Rae answered. She ran her finger over one of her eyebrows, smoothing it down.

"Then what? Explain it to me. You don't know me from a hole in the wall. Why are you so sure I didn't set the bomb?" Anthony asked.

"Shut up. We know you didn't do it," Jesse said.

"I know *you* know I didn't do it," Anthony told Jesse. Then he turned back to Rae. "But I don't get why you're here. And I really don't like the idea of getting help from somebody when I don't know what's in it for them."

"I just . . . You don't seem like someone who—"

She stopped and did the eyebrow-smoothing thing again.

"Bull," Anthony said. "Tell me the truth. Or get out. Jesse can talk to Nunan alone."

Rae didn't answer. She was quiet for so long, he started to think she was never going to. Then she let out a shaky breath. "Jesse, do you mind waiting outside for me?" she asked.

"Why?" Jesse asked, crossing his arms over his chest.

"I want to talk to Anthony alone for a minute, okay?"

Jesse looked over at Anthony, and Anthony nodded, then Jesse stood up reluctantly and headed for the door.

"This better be good," Anthony said.

Rae studied him for a moment, her blue eyes wary. "Oh, it's good. It's very good." She shifted in her chair, then grabbed her purse and pulled out a lipstick. She coated her mouth in a couple of quick moves, not going outside the line once.

"You need lipstick to talk about it?" Anthony asked, trying not to fixate on her mouth, now that it was all slick and shiny.

"I'm nervous, okay?" she snapped. She dropped the lipstick back in her purse, then cradled the purse on her lap. "You know I was in the hospital, right?"

"Yeah. You had some kind of breakdown," he answered. But what in the hell did that have to do with him?

"Yeah. I totally lost it. What happened was, I started getting all these thoughts in my head. Thoughts that weren't mine," she said in a rush, pressing her purse even closer to her body.

"What's that supposed to mean—not yours?" Anthony asked. Was the girl a total fruitcake? She'd seemed okay at Oakvale, but this was not sounding good.

"I can't explain it. The thoughts . . . I wasn't *thinking* them. They kind of just appear in my head. Sometimes clear. Sometimes fuzzy. Sometimes almost blocked out by static or something. And sometimes . . . sometimes they *feel* like other people. Like my dad. Or Jesse. Or . . . you." She gave a harsh laugh. "Don't think I don't know how this sounds. When you get out of here, you can organize a sanity hearing and testify against me."

Anthony kept his eyes on her face. He was good at telling when people were lying. Rae looked kind of freaked, but he didn't think she was making this up.

"What does all this have to do with why you've decided to take me on as a charity case?" If he could just keep her talking, maybe he'd come to some decision about what her deal was. Right now he couldn't help thinking they'd let her out of the hospital way too early.

"When I was in the bathroom, after the bomb went off, I got some of the thoughts, the not-me thoughts. That's what I call them. I have them so much, I needed a name for them. Anyway, one of the . . . the thoughts . . ." Her eyelashes fluttered down, blocking him from looking into her eyes. "It was about you. It was something like, 'They'll think Anthony did it.' It's like someone was framing you."

She raised her eyes back to his, her gaze intense. Like she was trying to tell if he believed her. Anthony struggled to keep his face expressionless.

"And later, in the nurse's office, I was holding that blue cup of water you gave me. And this time the thoughts weren't about you. The thoughts *felt* like you," Rae continued, almost pleading with him to believe her.

"You got thoughts that felt like me," Anthony repeated. He leaned his chair back on two of the legs. "What were they?" He wasn't completely sure he wanted to know.

Rae pulled a tin of Altoids out of her purse. "Want one?" she asked.

"I want you to answer my question," he told her.

Rae popped one of the mints in her mouth and ground it between her teeth. "Basically it was just that you . . ." She stopped while she put the Altoids tin back in her purse. Anthony felt like screaming with frustration, but he waited for her to go on. "I got thoughts that made it sound like you really cared about what happened to me," she said so softly that he had to strain to hear her. "That you were worried about me. And that you wanted to find out who did it."

Anthony let the front chair legs fall to the floor. This was freakin' bizarre.

"And you think they were really my thoughts? I mean, are you supposed to be some kind of mind reader or something?"

Rae gave a helpless shrug. "I have no clue where the not-me thoughts come from. Maybe they are just more insanity." She shook her head. "But it doesn't feel that way, especially lately. I'm starting to wonder if—I don't know, if I'm *not* crazy. Not imagining things. Because these thoughts—they really *feel* like they're coming from other people."

"Look, I—" Anthony cleared his throat. She looked so scared, so vulnerable. Almost the way she did after the bomb. "I did have some thoughts like that. Seeing you all pale and everything, it freaked me out. I wanted to do something for you. But I didn't know what to do. That's why I gave you the water. It was lame, but it was *something*."

"It was a lot," she murmured, sounding a lot shyer than she usually did.

Anthony scooted his chair closer to the table. "If you really believe these *thoughts,* then why'd you tell Rocha you saw me? You could have stopped all this right then."

Rae pushed her hair away from her face. "God, I wish that's what I'd done. But it would be pretty psycho of me to actually believe these thoughts are true, right? I mean, what kind of person . . . I *still* don't know if I'm just being a squirrel." She put her hands down on the table, sort of reaching out to him without quite getting close enough to touch.

"I get it," Anthony told her. He noticed that a few strands of her curly hair were glued to her forehead. She was getting the sweats. He was, too. This was mind-blowing. "Are you getting any of the thought things now, while we're talking?"

It was kind of like watching a train wreck. He couldn't stop pushing her, needing to know exactly what he was dealing with here.

"Yeah," she admitted.

"Tell me," Anthony urged.

"It's full of static. But it's like, 'Can't stand another day.' 'Better than being at home.' 'Have to get Tom some Dos Equis,' " Rae muttered.

Anthony felt a trickle of cold sweat run down the back of his neck.

"I've completely freaked you out, haven't I?" Rae stood up. "I don't know what I was thinking. How could you believe me? Most of the time I don't even believe myself." She turned and started to walk away.

"Have to get Tom some Dos Equis," he repeated. "That's weird."

Rae turned back to face him, her purse held in front of her like a shield. "Why is that weirder than anything else?" she asked.

"Because Dos Equis is the beer my stepdad drinks. And his name is Tom," Anthony explained.

"That is kind of weird. But typical. Lately, anyway. Look, I've got to go." She hesitated. "So is it okay with you if I help out Jesse?"

"Yeah. If you want," Anthony answered, half his mind still on the Tom / Dos Equis thing. He didn't know what he was supposed to think about Rae's "not-me" thoughts. But whatever else was going on with her, now he was convinced she wanted to help him.

Rae took one step, then hesitated again. "There was another thought I got in the bathroom that day," she admitted. She dropped her eyes to the ground. "I got the one about you being set up. But I also got one about me."

"What was it?" Anthony asked when she didn't continue.

She raised her eyes to his. "The other one . . . It said, 'Definitely kill Rae.' So, if I'm not insane, which is a total possibility, that I am insane, I mean—" She stopped, taking in a quick, sharp breath. "If I'm *not,* then whoever set you up was planning to kill me with that bomb."

Chapter 9

I know Rae's powers are developing. I can almost see it happening when I look at her.

I don't think she's realized that she is . . . becoming. She knows something is wrong. I'm sure of that. But she has no idea what she is already capable of.

Even I don't know exactly what form her powers have begun to take. But I will, perhaps even before Rae knows herself. I have to work fast. If Rae starts to use her powers before I figure out what they are, someone could end up dead.

* * *

Rae ducked into the bathroom—

I got my period. **I wonder if Vince!**

—instead of heading right to the cafeteria. If she was going to have a "spontaneous" Jeff encounter, which she was pretty damn sure she was, she wanted to brush her hair and put on some fresh lipstick.

Rae headed over to the sinks. She started trying to squeeze between two other girls so she could see a little patch of mirror. The girls immediately backed off, giving Rae a whole mirror to herself.

One of the benefits of being an out-of-the-closet psycho, Rae thought. But it bugged her that she'd never even seen the girls before. They were clearly freshmen—the fact was practically painted on their Clearasil-dotted foreheads—so there was no way they'd witnessed The Incident in the cafeteria last year. Still, they'd obviously heard all the gory details.

The freshies rushed through their primping and hurried out of the bathroom. "It's not contagious, you know," Rae muttered. One of the stall doors behind her swung open. *Oh, great, now somebody's heard me talking to myself,* she thought. She glanced over her shoulder and saw Lea heading toward her.

"What's not contagious?" Lea asked.

"You know. My insanity," Rae answered.

"Did someone say something to you?" Lea demanded. She looked ready to storm out into the halls and start kicking butt.

"No. Not really," Rae said. "It's just, you know, I can tell people aren't exactly *comfortable* when I'm around."

"Butt-head kind of people," Lea answered as she washed her hands. "Not your friends. Speaking of which. What's up with you being a no-show at lunch the last couple of days?"

Rae shrugged. So did Lea think it was in Rae's "best interest" to keep eating lunch with them, even if it wasn't good for her to show up at their parties? Rae had to bite back the comment.

"Let me guess. Marcus and Dori. I told them they shouldn't let you know that—" Lea stopped short.

"I don't need to be protected from stuff," Rae snapped. "I'm not going to lose it if everyone's not perfectly, sickeningly nice to me all the time." She noticed a faint blush on Lea's cheeks but rushed on. "You know what would have helped, though? If someone had given me a heads up. I would have liked a couple of minutes' warning."

Like from my supposed best friend, she added silently.

Lea nodded. "I should have said something. You're right. It's just that I told them to keep it a secret, at least for a little while. But Dori, the girl can't keep her hands off Marcus for a—" Lea stopped herself again. She took a step toward the door. "So are you coming?" she asked, her voice suddenly all cheery and peppy. "We can sit at a different table."

Rae flinched. "I brought my lunch," she said. "I

think I'm going to eat in the art room. I'm right in the middle of this painting."

"Oh. Okay. I know how you get when you're in artist mode," Lea answered, sounding the faintest bit relieved. "So I'll see you later," she added. She gave a little wave as she headed for the door.

Rae quickly brushed her hair and did some minor makeup repair, ignoring the not-her thoughts that buzzed through her brain. She hurried out of the bathroom and made straight for the stairwell. When she reached the door, she grabbed the knob—

/get lucky/

—then hesitated. Maybe she was being a little too eager. Nothing was less attractive. She'd figured that one out pretty fast when she'd first started playing the guy-girl game. It wouldn't kill Jeff to have to miss a day with her.

Although it might kill me, Rae thought. She'd been looking forward to her vacation to the land of normal all morning. Especially with all the Anthony stuff heating up, Rae needed a little bliss time. *Tomorrow,* she told herself. *Jeff doesn't need to know—*

Before she could finish the thought, the door swung open. And Jeff was grinning at her from the other side. He grabbed her by the wrist and pulled her into the stairwell, then shut the door behind them. "I made us a picnic," he told her.

"I can see that," Rae answered, staring down at the square of folded sheet loaded with food.

"And just in case you're wondering, no animals were harmed in the preparation of this lunch. Although I cut my finger when I was making the carrots." He showed her the Band-Aid on his pinkie.

"Poor baby," Rae said, falling into flirt mode.

"You could kiss it and make it better," Jeff suggested. He gave her an exaggerated leer.

Rae laughed. "I guess I could do that. Since you got the injury cooking for me." Then she took his hand and gave his finger a quick kiss.

The atmosphere in the stairwell became charged, like the way the air outside feels right before a thunderstorm. Rae's eyes found Jeff's, and they stared at each other for a long, dizzying moment. Then Jeff leaned forward, just a little. Rae leaned a little toward him. And somehow they were kissing.

I've known this guy for, like, four days, Rae thought as she slid her hands into his hair. *This is probably not the best idea.*

But it felt so good. Her whole world was his hands and her hands, and his mouth and her mouth. And that world was a wonderful place to be.

Rae spotted Jesse in the 7-Eleven parking lot as the bus pulled up across the street. *Show time,* she thought. The bus's doors wheezed open, and she climbed out, did a quick traffic check, then ran over to Jesse.

"So is that guy Nunan working today?" she asked when she reached him.

"Yeah," Jesse answered. "I could have just gone in and talked to him myself."

"Do you know him at all?" Rae asked, not bothering to lecture Jesse about why this wasn't something he should do alone.

Jesse shook his head. "Not really. I've seen him with Anthony a couple of times."

Rae peered through the window at the guy behind the counter. He was stroking his shaved head and giggling to himself. Unfortunately, he looked like the type who might have difficulty remembering a variety of things. "So you ready to do this?"

Jesse answered by heading to the door. He held it open for Rae, then they headed to the counter side by side. "Nunan," Jesse said. "How's it goin'?"

Nunan ran his hand over his head one more time, then peered at Jesse. "Do I know you, little guy?"

Rae saw Jesse's shoulders stiffen at the little-guy crack, but he let it go. "I hang here with Fascinelli sometimes. This is his new girlfriend." Jesse jerked his thumb at Rae.

Is he saying that because he thinks that will make

Nunan not worry about talking in front of me? she thought. *Or because he actually believes it? Because if he thinks I'm Anthony's girlfriend, Jesse and I are going to have to have a long talk.*

"Oh. I was hoping you were comin' in to meet me," Nunan told Rae. "Strange girls are always dropping by because they've heard the legend of the Nunan."

Rae managed not to snort as she took in his little potbelly pushing out his ancient Mr. Bill T-shirt. "I can understand that," she answered, playing the flattery card. "But actually Jesse and I had something we wanted to ask you."

"Shoot." Rick grabbed a handful of sunflower seeds from a bag behind the counter and crammed them all into his mouth.

"When you left the, um, package for Anthony in the Oakvale bathroom, did you notice anything strange?" Rae asked. "Because somebody left a bomb in there. It almost killed me. I'm still freaking out, and I really need to find out who put it there just so I can feel safe again." She figured Nunan might like helping out a damsel in distress. Lots of guys did.

Rick's forehead furrowed. "Sorry—I didn't go to Oakvale," he answered. He spit out a couple of sunflower seed shells. "Not everyone can shell them in their mouths," he explained to Rae. "It's all in the tongue."

Oh. My. God, Rae thought. "Huh," she commented. "Anthony said you left some weed for him in the girls' bathroom."

"Wait." Rick spit out a couple more shells onto the counter, then swept them onto the floor with his hand. "Yeah. I remember now. I gave the stuff to this guy in Anthony's support group. He was buying some, and he told me he'd make the delivery to Anthony. I knew Fascinelli would be dying for some. Which, by the way, he owes me the cash for."

"What guy?" Jesse asked.

"Um, I can't remember his name. I was kind of wasted," Nunan admitted. He giggled, and a couple of wet sunflower seeds came flying out of his mouth.

It seems to be kind of your perpetual state, Rae thought, taking in Rick's bloodshot eyes. "Do you remember what he looked like, at least?" she asked, trying to keep the impatience out of her voice.

"He was . . . I don't know. He was some dude," Rick answered.

"White? Black? Asian? Brown hair? Blond hair? I'm looking for anything here," Rae urged.

Rick spit out a few more shells. "I think he might have been wearing a green shirt."

"A green shirt," Rae repeated.

Nunan nodded. "Absolutely. Green. Or possibly blue. Something watery."

"O-kay. Well, thanks," Rae said. *Thanks for nothing. This little field trip was totally pointless.*

"Then he goes, 'Something watery,'" Rae said.

"Classic Nunan," Anthony answered. He leaned back in his chair until it was balanced on two legs. The guy supervising the common room frowned at him, and Anthony let the chair drop back to the floor.

"Jesse's going to ask around a little at our next group meeting," Rae continued.

"No. You can't let him do that," Anthony said, an electric jolt of fear running through his body. "There's a good chance the person who stashed the pot also set the bomb. If they were setting me up, they'd want me seen in the bathroom. Jesse asks the wrong person the wrong question, and he could get hurt." If somebody went after Jesse because of him, Anthony would have to smash his way out of here and start busting heads.

Rae's eyes widened. "I can't believe I didn't think of that. You're right. I won't let him," she said quickly. "But I think I already told Nunan too much."

"Not a problem." Some of the tension eased out of Anthony's body. "He doesn't have enough brain cells left to remember much. But be careful. Not everyone's a Nunan." He studied her face, trying to make sure she was taking what he said seriously. "Maybe both of you should just leave it alone."

"I'm not going to leave it alone," Rae shot back. "You wouldn't be in this place if it wasn't for me."

"I wouldn't be in this place if someone hadn't framed me," he corrected her, finally accepting that that was the truth. Yeah, Rae played a part in getting him here. But she hadn't put the evidence in his backpack. He lowered his gaze to the table. "Listen, there's something else I want to talk to you about."

Anthony hesitated. He felt kind of like an idiot bringing this up. Maybe it was just encouraging her to be delusional. But he'd been awake most of the night, going over what she'd told him about her not-me thoughts. In the morning he'd done some research—a first for Anthony Fascinelli—and come up with a theory. And even though a Bluebird had no business coming up with a theory of any kind, Anthony thought maybe, just maybe, he was right.

"You know how you were telling me about those not-you thoughts?" he continued. He shot a quick glance at her. Her face had kind of tightened up.

"Uh-huh," she answered, doing her purse-as-shield thing again.

"I was reading this book." Well, actually he'd gotten one of the volunteers in the detention center library to read it to him. He'd been slick, he thought.

He was pretty sure the woman hadn't realized that he was getting her to read it because it would take him a zillion years.

"A book," Rae repeated, her voice flat.

"Yeah, a book on psi abilities," Anthony answered, leaning close to her so no one would overhear and getting a whiff of that grapefruit stuff she wore. "It said there are people who can touch an object and know the history of it. I was thinking that your thing might be something like that. Not that you're getting history, exactly. But some kind of data."

"We should try to figure out what to do next," Rae said, ignoring him. "Maybe I could try Nunan again and manage to catch him when he's not wasted."

"He's pretty much always wasted," Anthony answered. He unzipped his backpack and pulled out a pencil. "Try touching this." He wasn't going to let her back away from this. It was too important. For both of them.

"It's not about touching. The thoughts come into my head, okay? It's not psi; it's just psychotic."

Anthony shook his head. "If you were sure it was just insanity, you wouldn't have told me about it. And you wouldn't be doing all this stuff to help me. You believe the thoughts mean something. Why are you so afraid of trying to figure it out?"

"I'm not afraid," Rae insisted. "I just think it's stupid."

"You'd rather go on walking around feeling sorry for yourself, poor little insane girl?" Anthony shot back. Rae looked like she wanted to slap him, but he didn't care. "The other day you said you got some thoughts that felt like me when you were holding that cup I got for you. And you had your hand on this table when you told me a thought that sounded exactly like one my mother would have had. When she came to visit me, she was sitting at this table, too. So it's not like it's totally impossible that you—"

"Have some kind of supergirl powers?" Rae asked sarcastically. But she snatched up the pencil.

Anthony watched her intently. Looking for what, he had no idea. "Are you getting anything?"

"Rot in hell," Rae said.

"Forget it. I was just trying to—" Anthony began.

"No. That's what I *got*. The not-me thought. 'Rot in hell,'" Rae answered.

Anthony's heart gave a slam against his ribs. "Okay, one of the guys stabbed another guy with that pencil the other day. So 'rot in hell'—that could be some kind of vibe or something from the fight."

"What else have you got?" Rae asked. She sounded bored, but Anthony could see the tension in her body. If she was feeling even half of what he was, she had a volcano going off in her right now. Fear and excitement and triumph were gushing through his veins.

Anthony tossed a deck of cards on the table. Rae snatched it up. "I'm right," she muttered.

"That's what you got? 'I'm right'?" Anthony asked. The lava inside him cooled. Maybe the rot-in-hell thing was a fluke. Maybe it was just how Rae was feeling about Anthony at that second. Because the guy he'd gotten the cards from was mega depressed. He spent all his free time sitting on his bed, playing solitaire. The guy didn't even go into the TV room or anything. Anthony doubted he ever thought he was right about anything.

"The weird thing is, the 'I'm right'—it felt like you." Rae flipped the deck of cards over in her hands. She gave a little jerk and dropped the cards.

"Did you get another one?" Anthony asked, leaning even closer.

Rae shoved her curly hair away from her face. "Yeah. I got another one, not an Anthony-flavored one this time. It was, 'I wish I was dead.' " Rae swallowed hard. "God, I could feel this *loathing,* this self-hating crap."

"That's exactly what I'd expect you to get," Anthony told her, his voice rising. He forced himself to keep it low. "But I don't get the 'I'm right' thing.

The cards aren't mine." He frowned, thinking. Then he sat up straighter. "But I was holding them," he said, his excitement returning. "And I was thinking about how I was right! Because you picked up something from the pencil!"

He felt like a Cardinal. A total friggin' Cardinal. Rae was getting all the thoughts of the different people who'd touched an object. But how? He looked down at her hands, watching as she drummed her fingertips nervously on the desk. Her fingertips. Suddenly a vague idea began to come into focus in his mind.

"We've got to try something else. Come on." Anthony scrambled up from the table. "Got to show my friend where the bathroom is," he told the common-room supervisor. He got a like-I-care nod. He rushed across the room, glancing quickly over his shoulder to make sure Rae was following him. She was, but she didn't look happy.

He led the way to the kitchen and peered through the little glass window in the door. Perfect. It was empty.

Anthony headed straight over to the dishwasher and yanked it open. "Pick up one of those spoons and tell me what you get," he ordered. The spoons had been touched by tons of people, but they were freshly cleaned. If he was right, she wouldn't be able to get anything from them.

"Nothing," Rae muttered, tossing the spoon down on the counter. "See, I told you I'm not super—"

"We're not done," he cut her off. He tried to clear his mind, then he picked up one of the clean spoons, still warm from the final cycle. *I'm freakin' brilliant,* he thought.

"Now, you take it from me and touch it right where I'm touching," Anthony told her. "But don't tell me what you get. *I'm* going to tell *you.*"

"What, are you psychic, too?" Rae muttered. But she took the spoon from Anthony.

"You got it?" he asked, tripping over his words in his eagerness.

"Yep," Rae answered.

"Okay, here's what your not-you thought was— 'I'm freakin' brilliant,'" Anthony said. "Am I right?"

"Yeah," she admitted, her eyes narrowing. "And it felt like you again." She rubbed her forehead, spoon still clutched in her fingers. "How did you do that?"

"I just want to try a few more things first. Humor me, okay?" Because he thought he had it nailed now. The whole thing. Not just that she was picking up people's thoughts. But *how* she was doing it.

"Touch the spoon someplace else," he told her. *Man, I sound like an excited little kid,* he thought. *I've got to get a grip.*

He watched as Rae moved her fingers to a new

171

spot on the spoon. She hesitated for a moment, then shook her head. "Nada."

Who's the freakin' Bluebird now? Anthony thought.

"Now for one more test," he said. *The dancing doughnuts won three flamingos,* he thought as he picked up another warm spoon.

Rae took it from him, putting her fingers at the bottom. "I'm not getting any—" she started to say, but he reached out and gently moved her hand to the part of the spoon he'd touched, ignoring the low-level sparks of electricity he felt as his fingers brushed against hers.

She looked at him in amazement, then slowly began to speak. "The dancing doughnuts—"

"Won three flamingos," Anthony said along with her. The spoon slipped from Rae's fingers and clattered to the floor. She stared at it for an instant, then bent to pick it up. About halfway down she seemed to change her mind and knelt next to the spoon.

Anthony crouched down beside her. "Are you okay?"

She didn't answer. She kept staring at the spoon.

"The doughnuts-and-flamingos thing—that's exactly what I was thinking when I touched the spoon," he explained. "But you had to touch the spoon exactly where I did to know the thoughts. So you get it, right? When you touch people's fingerprints, you pick up their thoughts, Rae. That's it. Your brain's not screwed up."

Rae squeezed her eyes shut. Anthony watched her helplessly. Finally he reached out and stroked her hair. It felt soft under his fingers. "You okay?" he asked again.

She opened her eyes, and he could see a film of tears on them. *Don't let her start bawling,* he thought.

"So I'm not crazy," Rae said, her voice trembling.

"No way. You're amazing," Anthony answered. "You're a . . . a fingerprint reader. No one's going to be able to keep a secret from you—not without wearing gloves all the time."

"Fingerprints," Rae whispered. "God, fingerprints."

She reached out and grabbed Anthony's hand. Then she matched her fingertips to his. He felt a sizzle, like a current had gone from her to him or him to her. His fingers began to burn with a cold fire as if his skin were pressed against dry ice instead of warm flesh.

Rae dropped his hand. "Did you get something?" Anthony asked.

"I . . . I have to go," Rae said, backing toward the door.

"What? Why?" Anthony asked. He could see that she was shaking. "What did you get? What's wrong?"

"Nothing. I just have to go." Rae turned and bolted.

Chapter 10

Rae slowly walked home from the bus stop, her hands jammed in the front pockets of her jeans. She didn't want her fingertips to accidentally brush up against anything. Not now. Her brain felt raw. Tender. When she'd touched Anthony, it was almost like she'd become him, like every thought she had was his thought. Like there was no Rae anymore for that one instant.

It had been overwhelming. She didn't just get a few clear thoughts and some static. She got hundreds of thoughts, layers and layers of them, but somehow she'd been able to take them all in, although most of them had faded now. All she had left were a few impressions and feelings. Longing for his father. Fear of what could happen to him at his trial. Triumph in figuring out what was really going on with Rae. Deep appreciation about what she was doing for him. Concern for her. It had been so intimate. So intense.

Rae shook her head as she turned onto her block, remembering back to the time when rolling around on a bed with Marcus had been the most powerful thing she'd ever experienced. It felt so long ago.

She cut across her front lawn, the too long blades of grass flicking around her ankles. When she got to the front door, she hesitated. Then she slowly pulled her hands out of her pockets. "Not going to be able to get in the house without touching something," she muttered. Her fingers shook as she reached into her purse and pulled out her key.

I hope that guy Nunan!

It was one of the not-her thoughts that felt like her, with some of the static in the background. So if Anthony was right—which seemed pretty damn likely, freaky as it was—she'd just touched a finger-print on the key and gotten a thought from the person who left the fingerprint. The thought they were having when they left a print.

Rae's heart gave a double-quick beat. That's why it felt like her. The key was hers. The fingerprint on the key was *hers*. So she was picking up the thought she had when she locked the door this morning.

Oh God. It was really true. It wasn't that she

hadn't believed Anthony. How could she not when he gave her proof? But it was like she'd only believed it with her mind, and now she was starting to accept it in her gut, in her bones.

She used the key to unlock the door, then reached for the doorknob. Her hand froze half an inch away from it. *Just do it,* she told herself, then she lightly ran her fingers over the metal.

/that bitch, Rae/she should be home/yummy Jeffy! meeting at three/back alive from the hell mouth/ make her pay/bald spot

She felt tears sting her eyes, just like they had when she was with Anthony. "I'm not insane," she whispered. "I. Am. Not. Insane." Because it all made sense now. The "yummy Jeffy" and "back alive from the hell mouth" thoughts felt like her because they *were* her. And it wasn't hard to figure out who had left the other fingerprint thoughts, even with the static buzzing behind them. "That bitch, Rae" and "make her pay"—those were from Jesse. Those were exactly the kind of thoughts he'd be having when he was getting ready to trash her room. And the other ones— dear old starting-to-go-bald Dad.

Anthony had nailed it. Rae felt like letting out a whoop of pure relief and pleasure. She felt like dancing down the street, telling everyone she saw that she was *not* a squirrel girl. But that kind of behavior was much too weird for Rae Voight, perfectly sane girl.

Instead Rae played the doorknob like a piano, touching the fingerprints like keys.

/that bitch. Rae/make her pay/*bald spot /bald spot/bald spot/yummy Jeffy/yummy Jeffy/*

She noticed that each thought got a little fuzzier every time she accessed it. Which made sense. Every time she touched a fingerprint, she probably smudged it a little. Rae reached up as high as she could. *I'm not crazy,* she thought as she touched the top of the door. She pulled her finger away, then immediately pressed it back in the same spot. The thought came right back at her—*I'm not crazy*—strong and clear with no static.

Rae added an I'm-not-crazy thought to the doorknob. She wanted them everywhere. That way every time she touched something, she could hear the amazing news. She pressed one finger onto the new fingerprint on the doorknob. It was clear, but there was static underneath it. *Maybe the static comes if there are a lot of old fingerprints already on,* Rae decided. *The doorknob has tons of fingerprints, but the top of the door probably only has that one.* She promised herself she'd check out the theory later. She'd probably figure out tons more stuff now that she knew what was going on. Now that she wasn't cuckoo!

Rae opened the door and rushed inside. She tossed her backpack—

/Jeff/

—on the sofa. Everything around her looked a little brighter somehow. She was okay. She was really okay. No, she was more than okay; she was, she was . . . freakin' *gifted*. That's what you called someone who was psychic . . . gifted.

Rae hurried down the hall to her dad's cramped little study. She wanted to play with her gift some more. *This is so amazing,* she thought as she sat down in her father's ergonomically correct chair and scanned the desk. What should she try first? Pencil, she decided. Her dad was a compulsive pencil tapper. Whenever he was thinking hard—tap, tap, tap. She picked up the closest one by the little pink eraser and ran the fingers of her free hand down the shiny yellow surface.

/not sure Rae's better/Arthur as Christ/she's keeping something from me/Melissa/

He's so anxious when he thinks about me, Rae realized. The thoughts carried a little of the emotion with them, and the muscles of her shoulders had tightened painfully with her father's worries. And when he thought about her mother, Melissa, the grief was still so raw, it was as if she'd died last week instead of years and years ago.

How can he still care about her so much after what she did? Rae thought. *How can he still love her?* Rae dropped the pencil. She decided not to try another one. It was as if her dad decided to read her diary—if she kept a diary. It didn't feel right to go rooting around in his head. And anyway, she'd probably just get more worries about her, more thoughts about his King Arthur junk, and—gag—more thoughts about how much he loved his perfect dead wife.

Rae stood up and wandered back into the living room. *I'll have to make sure that Dad knows I'm okay,* she thought. *I don't want him to have a stroke worrying about me.* But she definitely wasn't going to tell him the truth. A person who had been hospitalized for "paranoiac delusions" should not go around spouting off about how all she really had was this amazing ESP talent.

She flopped down on the couch and rested her head on the padded arm. Her thoughts kept returning to her dad, like a fly that kept landing on a doughnut no matter how many times you tried to shoo it away. The past months had clearly been almost as hellish for him as they had for her. And she hated that.

Back when she was a little girl—*Be honest,* Rae told herself. *It wasn't just back when you were a little girl. You did it until you were well into your twelfth year as a walking, talking example of the word* dork.

Anyway, back then, whenever she and her dad had a fight or it was his birthday or Father's Day or whatever, she'd make these little drawings and leave them in the pocket of his robe. She had a sudden urge to do that now.

"So what if it's dorky," she muttered as she stood back up and headed to her room. "He'll like it. And maybe it will make him relax about me a little." She went over to her desk and grabbed her drawing pad and a handful of markers, letting her old thoughts and the static wash through her. She studied the sheet of blank white paper for a moment, then she smiled and started to work, the markers squeaking away.

A few minutes later she had a caricature of her dad done up as King Arthur. *Hi, Dad,* she scribbled at the bottom. Then she ripped the sheet off the pad, folded it into quarters, and made her way to her father's room before she freaked out about exactly how geeky she was being.

"I'm not going to make a habit of this or anything," she mumbled as she walked over to her father's closet and slid open the door. She jammed the drawing in the pocket of his old plaid bathrobe, then started to turn away.

But her eyes locked on the cardboard box on the shelf above the clothes rod. It had some of her mother's stuff in it. Rae's dad had told her, well, actually he'd urged her, to look at it whenever she wanted to. She'd never even pulled the box off the shelf.

Fingerprints last a long time, Rae thought, a tickle of anticipation running down her spine, anticipation mixed with fear. *I might be able to get some of her thoughts. I could see for myself what she was really like. 'Cause I'm never going to get anything but the fairy tale from Dad.* She shifted from one foot to the other, debating. Should she? Did she really want to know? Whatever she found out was going to stay in her memory forever.

But she couldn't remember her mother's touch or her voice or the way she smelled. This was her chance to know a thought, actually feel one of her mother's feelings. How could she pass that up? Rae snatched the box—

/love you, Melissa/miss you/sweet/

—down and opened it before she could lose her nerve. She sat down cross-legged on the floor with the box in front of her and studied the contents. Gently she pulled out one of those old-fashioned perfume bottles with the little squeezy bulb on top.

Rae gasped as the first thought hit her.

/going to be a mother/

Her body felt light. Her blood felt . . . fizzy. Joy. She'd gotten an infusion of absolute joy. Rae closed her eyes, the feeling so intense, she felt like the floor was spinning beneath her.

Tears filled her eyes as the mother-flavored

emotion faded. *I was just a little speck, and she already loved me that much,* Rae thought.

But she was crazy. Remember that, Rae? She was crazy. And not just crazy in a nice I-see-leprechauns-and-unicorns way. Crazy in a horrible, vicious way.

Except what if she wasn't? What if she was just like Rae, but she never understood what was happening to her? The thought was like the blow of a hammer. It could be true. Rae'd been thinking she inherited some kind of mental disorder from her mom. But what if what she'd really gotten from her mother was her . . . psychic ability?

Poor Mom. Rae remembered how terrified she'd felt the first day she'd started getting the alien thoughts in her head. Of course people would have thought her mother was insane. Of course her *mother* would have thought the same thing.

Rae felt a burst of sympathy for her mother. Her heart actually ached. It was a stupid expression, but it was true. *I wish I could have told her,* Rae thought. *I wish I could have—*

And then it hit her. How could she have forgotten for even a few moments? Her mother—the woman who Rae's heart was getting all mushy and achy over—had done something too horrible to imagine. And even if she did have Rae's fingerprint power, that was no excuse. There *was* no excuse.

The pleasure—the *joy*—she'd felt when she'd touched her mother's fingerprint drained out of her, like dirty water going down the drain. She went all numb inside. Which was just as well. Because if she wasn't numb, she'd hurt so bad, she might never be able to stop crying.

Rae dropped the perfume bottle back in the box and closed the lid as quickly as she could, then she jammed the box back onto its shelf and closed the closet door.

Rae didn't even consider going to the caf when the bell rang for lunch the next day. She went straight to the stairwell. She needed her Jeff fix—and right now.

Her *gift*, the gift she'd been so thrilled about yesterday, wasn't feeling quite so much like a gift today. Because now she knew that there were people—people right here in her school—who thought of her as a complete freak or at least some kind of damaged girl interrupted. It had been bad when those thoughts were flying around in her head unexplained. But the explanation, well, it wasn't exactly comforting. *At least you're not insane,* Rae reminded herself. *But you're not normal, either,* she couldn't help adding.

The stairwell door swung open, and Jeff appeared. He looked at her. She looked at him. And it was like suddenly their bodies were magnetized. Rae wasn't sure who took the first step, but an instant later they were in each other's arms. An instant after that, they were kissing, a sweet, soft kiss that made her feel warm all over, as if she were wrapped in a big fluffy towel straight out of the dryer.

Somehow, Rae wasn't sure exactly how because she definitely wasn't in control of her own body, they managed to lower themselves to the hard cement floor. They sat down on the top step without breaking the kiss.

Jeff flicked his tongue across her lips, and she eagerly parted them, allowing the kiss to deepen. She loved the taste of him. The feel. Warm and wet.

"Yummy, Jeff," she murmured into his mouth. He laughed, which made Rae start laughing, too. They struggled not to break the kiss, their mouths slipping and sliding across each other's but always keeping some kind of lip-to-lip contact.

Jeff slid one hand down her arm, then wrapped her hand in his. *Closer,* Rae thought, too delirious to form sentences anymore. *Want closer.*

She maneuvered her fingertips until they were resting on top of Jeff's. And a tidal wave of his thoughts rushed over her, overwhelming her.

/knew she'd be easy/loser girls are grateful for it/probably would have gone down on day one/nice little setup/no demands/oh God/yes/

She jerked away, ripping her lips off Jeff's. "What's the problem?" he demanded.

Rae sprang to her feet, swallowing hard. "Let me ask you something," she said, forcing herself to sound calm, firm. *Normal*.

Jeff stood up and gave her a lazy smile. "Don't tell me you're suddenly worried about how I really feel about you. You've got to know we feel the same way. We just clicked from the second—"

Rae shook her head. "That's not what I was going to ask." Fury pumped through her veins, but she kept her voice even. "My question is—what kind of a guy would only want to fool around with a girl he thought was a loser?"

"What?" Jeff gave a rapid couple of blinks.

"I mean, I don't have a degree in psychology or anything, but don't you think a guy who thinks only a loser girl would want him—wouldn't you think that guy would have to be pretty much of a loser himself?"

"Um, I guess so," Jeff muttered.

"I guess so, too." Rae walked out of the stairwell without another word and headed down the hall toward the bathroom. She felt like taking a shower, a long, long shower, but she'd have to settle for washing her hands.

She ripped open the bathroom door, ignoring the thoughts and static, and rushed over to the sinks. Lea stood by the nearest one, drying her hands with one of the thick paper towels.

"We have to stop meeting like this," Lea said when she saw Rae. She tossed the paper towel in the big metal garbage can, gave a little wave, and headed for the door. "See you later," she called.

"Okay," Rae answered, glad Lea hadn't decided to stay for a little nicey-nicey chat. She couldn't deal with that right now. She turned on the cold water at the closest sink.

/glad Rae didn't show at lunch/

Rae recognized the flavor of that thought immediately. It was Lea all the way. The hairs on the back of her neck stood up. And Rae realized the little frisson of fear she was feeling was Lea's fear.

Lea's fear of Rae.

Rae stared at herself in the mirror, taking in her big eyes and pale face. *I'm never going to be the same,* she realized. *I'm never going to be able to walk around feeling like people are basically decent. I'm always going to know what's going on underneath. I'm always going to see the fear and the hate and the . . . the slime.*

At that thought she felt something die inside her. The little bit of Rachel she had left, the Rachel who drew unicorns and almost believed in them.

It's better to know the truth, Rae told herself. *About Lea. About Jeff. About everybody.*

Including whoever it was out there in the world who wanted her dead. Rae'd been trying not to think about that. Like if she just pretended it wasn't happening, it would go away.

That's not going to happen. Another piece of truth you have to face. So brush the sand out of your hair, ostrich girl, and decide what you're going to do. Are you going to stand around and wait for whoever it is to come after you again? Or are you going to be the one who makes the decisions?

ae stood at the bus stop near the police station, peering down the street. She saw a bus coming toward her, shimmering in the heat. "You better be on that bus, Jesse," she muttered. She checked her watch. He was already five minutes late. Rae couldn't believe it. It felt more like five hours.

The bus groaned to a stop in front of her. Jesse was the first one out, pushing his way in front of a couple of blue-haireds, who did not look at all pleased with this example of a young southern gentleman. "Let's go, already," Jesse urged, as if he'd been the one waiting for *her.*

They did a speed walk—minus the geeky arms— to the police station. "First thing we have to do is find out where the evidence room is," Rae said. She followed Jesse through the door, grateful she didn't have to touch it herself. The cocktail of thoughts she'd get off that door would probably not be at all pleasant.

"I'll handle it," Jesse said. Without bothering to explain how, he started right for the main desk. Rae hung back. She didn't think the guy at the desk, the one with the bad comb-over, would remember her, but it seemed stupid to risk it. A few seconds later Jesse was back. "Second floor, a little ways down from the elevator on the right," he said.

"What? You just went up and said, 'Hi, what floor is the evidence stored on'?" Rae asked as they headed to the elevator.

"No," Jesse answered, sounding disgusted. "I told him my cousin is working the evidence room today and he told me to stop by so he could give me the ten bucks he owes for our grandmother's birthday present."

"Not bad," Rae told him. She let him push the elevator up button and then the button for the second floor. There were some things she just had no real desire to know. *Maybe I'll have to be like some of the old ladies who still wear white gloves,* Rae thought.

"My turn," she said as the elevator doors opened. She took a deep breath, then stepped out, Jesse right behind her. Without hesitation she strode down the hall. She saw something that looked kind of like a bank teller window. It had a short counter running in front of it, with a sign-in sheet and pen lying there. "Hi," Rae said to the guy behind the window. "Someone told us there was a soda machine up here."

The guy shook his head. "First floor," he answered.

Rae smiled at him, looking him straight in the eye. "Thanks," she said as she pulled out a stick of gum and managed to accidentally-on-purpose drop it on the guy's desk. "I got it," she said, before he could move. She leaned through the window and ran her fingers over as much of his desk as she could with her left hand—

/Alan fighting at school/friggin' paperwork/talk to Alan/stop at cash machine/kid can't even handle sixth grade/buy bread/call Alan's teacher/

—as she reached for the gum with her right. "Come on," she told Jesse as she started back to the elevator.

"Did you get anything?" he whispered when they were out of sight.

"Enough, I think," Rae answered. She couldn't believe how casually Jesse asked her that question, like he knew dozens of people who could pick thoughts off fingerprints. Or like it was something minor she'd revealed about herself—like that auburn wasn't her natural hair color.

He'd had questions, of course, when she'd told

him the truth, figuring he needed to know if they were going to come up with the best-possible plan. And he'd made her touch about a hundred of his fingerprints as proof. But then he'd been kind of like, "Okay, cool," as if she were one of the X-Men or something.

"So now what?" Jesse asked.

Rae thought for a minute, glad that the hallway was still empty. "Can you sound any older on the phone?"

"Definitely," Jesse answered, deepening his voice. And he actually did sound reasonably grown-up.

"Okay, here's what you do. Go downstairs and call up to the evidence room. Ask for Walter Child. That's the guy's name. I saw it on his desk. Anyway, tell him you're calling from the school and that his son Alan got in a fight. Tell him you need him to come over right away to pick Alan up and take him home because he's not going to be allowed to leave without a parent," Rae said. "That should get him out of the room for a few minutes—even if he just goes to find someone to cover for him. I'll sneak in and—"

"I know the plan, remember?" Jesse interrupted.

"Sorry," Rae said. "I'm just a little nervous."

"I'll come back up as fast as I can," Jesse promised.

"No," Rae told him. "We can't both get caught.

You have to be my backup. If something happens to me, I'll need you free to deal with it."

"All right," Jesse said, a little reluctantly. "I'm takin' the stairs. The elevators are too slow." He turned and rushed out the door leading to the staircase. Rae positioned herself near a drinking fountain that was out of the sight line of the evidence guy.

Now she just had to wait and see if Mr. Walter Child would take the bait. It didn't take long. About three minutes after Jesse hit the stairs, Rae heard a door open down the hall. She spun toward the drinking fountain and leaned over it, letting her long hair curtain her face. When footsteps neared her, she allowed herself one quick peek. *Yep. There goes Walty,* she thought.

As soon as he was through the door to the stairs, she bolted down to the evidence room. She figured there was a buzzer that would open the door next to the window, but she didn't see it. So she looked both ways down the hall to make sure it was still empty, then scrambled through the window. She landed on all fours on the desk, then half jumped, half fell to the ground.

Rae crouched in front of Walter's computer and managed to find the database that detailed each case. She typed in Anthony's name, ignoring the thought fragments she picked up, and seconds later she had the number of the bin where the evidence for his case was held. *Thank God it was a fast modem,* she thought. Staying low, she hurried across the little office and through the back door. Rows of long metal shelves filled the large storage area.

"Pretty much like using the library," Rae muttered as she spotted the cards at the end of each row that indicated the bin numbers. She trotted down the row that had Anthony's number, found the bin, which was just your basic box, and opened it. A bunch of junk that looked like it could make a bomb was inside. "Bingo," she said, slipping into geekspeak in her nervousness.

Rae ran her fingers across the handle of the pliers—

Iget me a motorcyclelwhy want to kill Raelhope it doesn't explode in my facel

the tissue paper—

Igot to buy a diamond belly ringlgonna be loadedlFascinelli would have gotten busted for something eventually, anywayl

and the wooden stick—

Imaybe take off for Mexicolthat new girl, Raelbut I'm not really the murdererl

Rae heard the door that led from the office swing open. "It's me. Jesse," a voice called, low and anxious.

"I told you not to come in here," she answered.

"The guy . . . He's coming back. . . . I think he

called his wife to check," Jesse said, breathless. "We have to get out of here. Now."

Rae didn't need to be told twice. She slammed the top back on the box and ran. Jesse fell into step behind her. "You get enough?" he demanded.

"Hope so," she answered.

"So our guy is into motorcycles. Knows Rae's new in group. Probably has a girlfriend with a pierced navel. And likes Mexico." Anthony glanced at Jesse, who was in his usual chair at their usual table in the visitors' room.

We're regulars already, Rae thought.

"Sound like anyone we know?" Anthony asked Jesse.

"David Wyngard," Jesse answered. "All he ever talks about is motorcycles."

"And Cynda," Anthony added. "She has piercings everywhere."

"Wait. Cynda, which one is she?" Rae asked.

"She's in our group, too. You know. Dyed black hair. Wears those army camouflage pants a lot," Jesse answered.

Rae knew exactly who he was talking about. "That's who told me to go into the bathroom the day the bomb went off," she exclaimed. "She said I had to fix my lipstick or something. God, she wanted to make sure I was in place at exactly the right time."

"So, it's gotta be David," Anthony said. "That jerk. I can't believe he framed me. We're supposed to be friends. Sort of."

"I did get a thought where he was telling himself you'd get caught for something eventually, anyway," Rae offered.

"Yeah. I go around trying to kill people every couple of days," Anthony muttered.

"I still don't get why he—or Cynda—would want to off Rae," Jesse said.

"You mind keeping your voice down a little?" Anthony asked, with a glance toward the guy supervising the room. "I don't know why, but for some reason, they don't really like us to talk about offing people during visiting hours."

"Sorry," Jesse said, a faint blush creeping up the back of his neck. "But like I said, I don't get it."

"Me neither," Rae added. "I'd never even seen either of them before my first day at group, so it's not like they have something against me."

"But it was all about you; that's what you picked up," Anthony said.

"Yeah," Rae answered.

Anthony ran his fingers through his hair. It was a little greasy and a little long, and it definitely gave him that bad-boy look. "We shouldn't bother trying to figure it out until we're positive David's the right guy. It's not as if liking motorcycles is all that unusual."

"I'll bring him to the 7-Eleven after group tomorrow," Jesse volunteered. "Nunan can get a look at him."

"Sounds like a plan," Anthony agreed.

"What about Cynda?" Rae asked. "She could've been in on it."

"Probably not," Anthony answered. "Even though she dresses like G.I. Jane, she's kind of a wuss. One time I saw her make David catch a spider and put it out the window. She didn't want it near her. But she didn't want him to kill it, either."

"If I get Nunan to ID David, then we can worry about the Cynda thing," Jesse said. "He might not even be our guy."

"I'll go with you tomorrow," Rae told Jesse.

"No," Anthony and Jesse said together.

"You don't even know David, and it's not like you and Jesse have been buds or anything. It'll be too suspicious if you try to tag along," Anthony explained. "Jesse's hung out with me and David a few times at the 7-Eleven. It won't be weird for him to maneuver David over there."

Rae nodded reluctantly. It made sense. But she wasn't all that happy with the idea of Jesse and the potential wanna-be killer drinking a Slurpee together.

"You guys should go. My mom might be stopping

by, so . . ." Anthony let his words trail off. It was obvious he didn't want them meeting his mom.

What is he embarrassed about? she wondered. She couldn't imagine anyone whose mom wasn't a *murderer* like hers actually caring. She would give anything for a mom who just talked a little too loudly or gave her big hugs in front of her friends. But there was no way she'd let Anthony, Jesse—or anyone— know the real truth about *her* mom.

Rae sighed, standing up alongside Jesse.

"See you later," Jesse said.

"Bye," Rae mumbled. She started to say something else, some kind of thank-you, but everything she thought of sounded lame, so she just followed Jesse out of the room. About halfway out of the detention center she decided she was being a total wimp.

"I, um, forgot my sunglasses," she blurted out to Jesse. "I'll be right back." Without waiting for an answer, she turned and ran back to the visitors' room. She wasn't sure if she was happy or not when she saw that Anthony was still at their table.

Oh, show some ovaries, she told herself. She hurried over to the table and started speaking without bothering to sit down. "I just wanted to say thanks," she told him. "What you did for me—God. Do you even know?"

Anthony stared up at her, his expression unreadable.

Rae sat down and leaned toward him. "When I was having all those, you know, not-me thoughts, I figured I was going totally insane. I mean, they're why I ended up in the hospital. To know that I'm . . ." She swallowed hard and rushed on, her words crashing into each other. "To know that I'm okay, sane, it changes my whole life. And you did that for me." She stood up fast. "So, that's it. Thanks."

She bolted without waiting for Anthony's reaction.

Chapter 12

Anthony watched Jesse head across the visitors' room the next day. He could tell just by looking at the kid's face that the 7-Eleven plan had worked. Jesse looked like he'd swallowed a lightbulb or something.

"David's the guy Nunan gave the pot to," Jesse whispered as he swung himself into his usual chair. "We've got him."

This has nothing to do with him. But he's acting like he's the one something great happened to, Anthony thought. Jesse had been pretty friggin' amazing during this whole thing. He'd believed in Anthony 100 percent, which Anthony's own mother definitely couldn't manage.

"We've got something," Anthony agreed. He didn't want to make Jesse feel like a loser. But he didn't want Jesse to think everything was all fine, either. That would be treating him like a baby, and if Jesse was anything like Anthony—and he was, sort of—nothing would make him more ticked off.

Jesse's eyes darkened. "What do you mean? David's goin' down. And you're gettin' out of here."

Bible Bob strolled over to the table before Anthony could explain. "It's nice to see you getting so many visitors," he told Anthony. "Not everyone does." He rested his hand on Jesse's shoulder. "Is this one of your brothers?"

"Nope," Anthony answered. "He's just a bud."

"Yeah," Jesse muttered, not sounding too happy.

"An honorary brother kind of bud," Anthony added. Jesse smiled, a smile so big, it hurt Anthony to look at.

"That's the best kind to have," B. B. said. He glanced at his watch. "You guys will need to wrap it up in about five minutes. Anthony's group is setting up the dining room tonight," he explained to Jesse. Then with a half salute he wandered off.

"So what'd you mean about us having *something?*" Jesse asked as soon as B. B. was out of earshot.

"It's not like we can just tell the cops that David set off the bomb," Anthony explained. "There's no way they'd believe it without proof."

"Is that it?" Jesse looked extremely pleased with himself. "Not a problem, bro. Rae's getting proof right now."

"Wait. Where is she?" Anthony demanded, adrenaline starting to slam through his body.

"She's at David's," Jesse answered. "I found out that David was going over to Cynda's after he left the 7-Eleven. I told Rae, and she said she was going to go search his place. I wanted to go in with her, but she said there would be less chance of getting caught with one person, so I just told her where it is. Then I came straight here."

"I can't believe her," Anthony muttered, fury and fear building inside him. "David tried to *kill* her. And she's just going to go strolling into his house?" He felt his heart squeeze into a hard ball in his chest. "You have to go stop her," he ordered Jesse.

Jesse's eyes widened. "It's way too late."

"Oh, great," Rae muttered when she saw the car in David's driveway. She and Jesse had been so psyched at having a little stretch of time when they were sure David would be out that they hadn't even thought about anybody else in his family.

Rae shook her head. She wasn't turning back. There had to be a way. All she needed was someone to distract whoever was home at David's while she did her search. She snatched up her cell phone, tuning out her old thoughts, and dialed Jesse's number. No answer.

Who else? Who else? She realized she was standing right in front of David's house, staring. Not too bright. She turned and walked away at a casual stroll. *Just out on a little walk, everybody,* she thought. *No need to alert the neighborhood watch.*

Her fingers tightened around the cell phone. Who else? Not Marcus, that was for damn sure. And not Lea. Lea was already afraid of her. If Rae called her, babbling about needing backup on some secret info-gathering mission, she'd flip out.

Who else? A name sprang into her mind. Yana. In a way they didn't know each other nearly well enough for Rae to be dragging her into this. But she was the only one, other than the not-home Jesse and the locked-away Anthony, who Rae trusted enough.

She didn't give herself time to debate. When she turned the corner, moving out of sight of David's house, she just dialed. Yana picked up on the second ring. Rae gave her the rundown as quickly as she could—how she and Jesse had found out some stuff that convinced her Anthony really had been framed for that bomb, and now she just needed to get the evidence that could clear him. She didn't mention the fingerprints stuff. She was still weirded out that

Anthony and Jesse knew. And she really, really wanted a friend, one friend, who she could just be normal with. Yana was cool about the hospital. But that didn't mean she was into the psychic friend thing.

"So what do you think?" Rae asked, wrapping up her story. "Are you up for it?"

"Are you kidding?" Yana exclaimed. "I always wanted to be a Charlie's Angel."

Rae knew better than to thank Yana. She'd already figured out Yana hated that. "I'm on the corner of Madison and Winchester. It's—"

"I know where it is, I'm there." Yana hung up without saying good-bye.

Rae kept the phone to her ear, trying to look like she was in the middle of an important call, just in case anyone was wondering what she was doing hanging around in the neighborhood without even a dog to walk or anything.

She didn't have to wait long. About ten minutes later Yana's yellow Bug came flying around the corner. Not exactly inconspicuous, but hey, at least Yana was there. That counted for a lot.

Yana parked and jumped out of the car. "I have a plan," she announced before Rae could say anything. "Take me to the house."

"Do I get to hear this plan of yours?" Rae asked as she led the way back around the block.

"Nope. You have to trust me." Yana grinned.

Rae couldn't help but grin back. "It's hard not to trust someone in a Happy Burger uniform."

"I actually work there, if you can believe it," Yana answered, staring down with disgust at the big purple smiling face button pinned to her collar. "I put this on because I thought it would be a good disguise. Generic and all."

"Crafty," Rae said. "But really—the plan? What is it?"

"You gotta trust me. I told you. I just need to know if this guy David has a girlfriend," Yana said.

"Yeah. Her name's Cynda," Rae answered. Even without knowing the plan, she was starting to feel confident she and Yana were going to make this work somehow. It was that Yana vibe kicking in. The girl was nothing if not confident.

"That's all I need," Yana said.

"Good. 'Cause we're here." Rae jerked her chin toward a cozy little house with gingerbread trim. It looked too sweet for a wanna-be killer to live in.

"Just whatever I say, don't disagree with me," Yana instructed as she led the way up the flagstone path and gave a double knock on the door. A woman with yellow hair—*yellow*—opened the door. Rae figured she had to be David's mother. Yana's bottom lip started to tremble the second Mrs. Wyngard looked at her. "Where is he? Where's David? You have to tell me," she pleaded.

A frown line appeared between Mrs. Wyngard's eyebrows. "He's not home," she answered. "Is there something I can do for you?" Mrs. Wyngard was clearly hoping Yana would say no. Instead Yana pushed her way into the house, dragging Rae behind her.

"Well, we're going to need a car seat. And some bottles and stuff. And Pampers," Yana rattled off.

"What?" Mrs. Wyngard cried. "Pampers? What?"

Yana put her hands on her hips. "He didn't tell you, did he? He promised me he would. And he promised he'd go shopping with me today to pick out a cradle. But he never showed up." She let out a wail that Rae was sure could be heard for blocks.

"Are you telling me—" Mrs. Wyngard began.

"I'm telling you you're going to be a grandma. In about seven months," Yana interrupted. "And that girl Cynda. She's history."

Rae choked back a burst of hysterical laughter. Yana was amazing.

"I'm sorry. What's your name?" Mrs. Wyngard asked, sounding dazed.

"It's—oh God. I think I have to puke again. Where's the bathroom?" Yana burst out.

"First door on the right," Mrs. Wyngard answered, pointing to the hall.

"Come with me," Yana told Rae. She grabbed Rae by the sleeve, and they flew down the avocado-colored carpet and into the bathroom. Rae shut the door behind them. "Do you think you could get me some soda crackers, Grandma Wyngard?" Yana called, plopping down on the fuzzy purple toilet seat.

There was a muffled sound from the hall that sounded like half a yes and half a moan. "I'll stay here and make puking sounds," Yana whispered. "You go search David's room. She'll think you're still with me."

Rae cracked open the door, checked the hall, then crept out. She tiptoed to the next door, feet silent on the carpet, and took a fast look into the room. It was a sty. *This has to be the place,* she thought. She ducked into David's room and closed the door—

/Cynda and me/

—behind her. God, where to start first. Under the bed, she decided. She grimaced as she stretched out on her stomach on David's carpet. There were dirty clothes everywhere, and they all had that funky over-ripe guy-who-badly-needs-a-shower smell. She jammed both hands under the bed and felt around.

/get condoms/dog food/friggin' group therapy/

Nothing useful. Rae shoved herself to her feet and took another look at all the crap. There was a Coke can on David's dresser that seemed out of place. Only because it was standing upright in the midst of a pile of junk. On impulse, she headed over to it. She'd seen a Coke can in a joke store once that was fake—it twisted open in the middle. She could see David as the kind of guy who would think that was cool.

Using the very tips of her fingers, Rae twisted on the can. It opened. And there was a stash of gray powder inside. She took a sniff. Yes! Gunpowder. Rae closed the can. Lightly, very lightly so she wouldn't leave any fingerprints of her own, Rae stroked the can.

tons o' cash/get out of here/won't ever get caught/

That's what you think, bud, Rae thought. She slipped the can into her big canvas bag, which she'd emptied out for evidence gathering.

"I have the crackers," she heard Mrs. Wyngard call from down the hall.

"Leave them outside the door, please," Yana answered. "And if you have some 7UP, I think that would really help." Loud ralphing sounds followed. Then Rae heard footsteps heading away from the bathroom—and David's room. *Thank you, Yana,* she thought, *even though you don't want to be thanked.*

Rae did a quick dresser drawer search. They were almost empty, which was no surprise since it seemed like every article of clothing David owned was on the floor. She crouched down and checked under the dresser. There was half a dog bone and a partially chewed-up piece of wood. Wood that looked like the same size as the piece that had been with the pipe bomb stuff. With a sigh Rae got down on her stomach again. She slid her arm into the tight space under the dresser and snagged the wood with her fingertips.

I hope I really know how to do this!

As she pulled her hand back out, it snagged on something rough. "Damn it," Rae muttered. "That took off a layer of skin." She let go of the piece of wood, curious what she'd gotten caught on. It looked like a ragged piece of floorboard. She gave it an experimental tug, and a thin piece of wood came away in her hand.

"I feel another bingo coming on," Rae whispered, her stomach feeling like it had gotten onto a down elevator, one that was moving with superspeed. She twisted onto her side, then wriggled her fingers into the little hole that had been hidden by the wood. She felt something soft against her skin. *Maybe it's more of the tissue paper,* she thought. She managed to squeeze a clump of the paper between two of her fingers, then she pulled it out of the hole.

It wasn't tissue paper. It was money. A whole wad of hundred-dollar bills. Rae pulled the money free. Then she ran her fingers lightly across the metal of the heavy silver money clip.

An involuntary gasp escaped her throat. She hadn't been expecting this. None of them had.

* * *

Rae didn't get up from the park bench when she saw Anthony walking toward her. It was just a little too weird seeing him here. Not in the detention center. Not in the group. Just in your basic real life.

"Hey," he said.

"Hey," Rae said back. "You going to sit down or what?" The words came out kind of surly sounding, as if she didn't want him to get anywhere near her. Which wasn't true. At least it mostly wasn't true. It was just that this guy knew way too much about her.

You know stuff about him, too, she reminded herself as he stiffly took a seat. *Like how he feels about his dad.*

"Jesse's not here yet?" Anthony asked, sounding equally uncomfortable.

"No. I mean, do you see him?" Rae asked. God, she was being a bitch. And Anthony definitely didn't deserve that. But besides being nervous around him, she was still creeped out by what she'd found at David's house.

"That stuff you sent to Ms. Sullivan worked fast," Anthony commented. He rested one arm along the back of the bench, then immediately lowered it back to his side.

"Yeah. Well, I'm sure the cops figured out that the wood and the gunpowder were the same," Rae answered. "Plus David's hands were all over the money and everything else. I told them to check the fingerprints in the note I put in the envelope."

"We have to figure out a way to prove that David was really trying to kill you," Anthony said. "He'll probably get put in youth prison for the bomb. But he'll get out—and not all that long from now. You're not going to feel safe when that happens."

The discovery she'd made at David's hit her full force again. But she wasn't going to mention it to Anthony. It wasn't his problem. She'd helped put him in the detention center, and she'd helped get him out. They were all even now. And that's how she liked it.

"I'm not trying to freak you out or anything," Anthony added. "It's not like you'll have to worry about David right away. It's just something we should be thinking about."

"I'm not worried about it," she told him, shooing a bee away from her face. Why had she even agreed to meet up with him and Jesse for this little celebration? It was ridiculous. She had much more important things to do. Like figure out how to save her life.

"You're not worried about it," Anthony repeated.

"Look, I'll handle it when I have to handle it," Rae said sharply. "And I won't need any help to do it."

Anthony shoved his hands in his pockets. "Okay. I get it. You can run along now. You wouldn't want one of your prep school friends to see you with me and Jesse."

"Oh, please," Rae muttered. "Get dramatic, why don't you. Like you said, David's going to jail. So I don't have to worry about—"

"Bull," Anthony interrupted. "You have to be scared crazy at the thought that the guy who tried to kill you is going to be wandering free in Atlanta in a few months. But you hate the idea of spending one more second around a guy like me, so much that you're willing to risk getting killed instead of letting me help you." He picked her backpack up off the ground and thrust it toward her. "Here. Don't bother waiting for Jesse. You don't have to do us any favors."

Rae didn't pick up the backpack. She stared at Anthony until he reluctantly met her gaze. "Aren't you gone yet?" he asked.

"Don't do you any favors? Is that what you said?" Rae's voice got louder with every word. "What have I been doing all this time except friggin' favors for *you?*"

"Just because you felt guilty," Anthony shot back. "Which you should have. Because if you hadn't opened your big mouth—"

"This again?" Rae sprang to her feet. "You know what? I think I will take your advice just this once. I'm outta here." She grabbed her backpack.

/FREAKIN' CARDINAL GIRL/

Rae spun back to face Anthony. "What's a Cardinal girl? Is that some kind of code or something?"

Anthony's head jerked slightly, like he'd been slapped. "Keep your fingers out of my head, you mutant," he barked.

Mutant. That's what he really thinks. Of course he does. Marcus. Lea. Jeff. They all think I'm a loser or some kind of scary freak. And they don't even know about the fingerprint thing. Why should Anthony be any different with everything he knows about me?

Rae pulled on her backpack, ordering herself not to cry. She got only one step away from the bench before Anthony snagged her by one of the straps and hauled her back.

"You said you wanted me to leave. Now you won't let me," Rae muttered, turning toward him again.

"I don't think you're a mutant," he confessed. His voice was harsh, but his eyes searched her face as if he was actually worried he'd hurt her.

"You said it. You must have meant it," Rae answered.

"You going to believe what I said? Or you going to believe what I thought?" Anthony asked. He raked his hands through his hair. "A Cardinal girl is, you know, one of the elite." He used the toe of one sneaker to wipe a spot of mud off the other one. "You know, smart, pretty, classy. All that."

"Oh," Rae muttered. She knew he meant it. She just wasn't sure what to say in response. *You can't let him go on believing that you wouldn't want to be seen with him because you're so special, because you're a Cardinal and he's a Bluebird or whatever he called himself that day at Oakvale.*

Rae reached out and gave Anthony's sleeve a little tug as she searched for the words. "It's not that I'm embarrassed to hang out with you—or Jesse. But there's no reason for either of you to get all involved with my problem. I mean, it's not something you need to take responsibility for. It's not like me getting you sent to the detention center. You didn't have anything to do with—"

"You think I'm just going to walk away and let some maniac come after you because it's not my problem?" Anthony sounded outraged. "What the hell do you think I am? Anyone who would do that doesn't deserve to take up space." He sat back down and slapped the spot on the bench next to him. Rae hesitated, then sat back down, too. It would be so good not to have to go through this alone. And even though she'd known him only a couple of weeks, Anthony was definitely the guy she'd want at her back.

"So are we going to come up with a way to prove David tried to kill you or what?" Anthony asked.

"It's not David we have to worry about," Rae

admitted, relieved at the chance to let out her secret, to stop holding this terrifying thing inside her.

"Then who?" Anthony asked, his dark brown eyes intent.

Rae pulled a small paper bag out of her purse. With her fingertips she removed a silver money clip. "I found this at David's. It was holding together a wad of cash. When I touched it . . ." Rae heard her voice tremble a little. She pulled in a deep breath, trying to keep it together.

"When you touched it . . ." Anthony prompted.

"I got a thought from David," Rae admitted. "Anthony, somebody *paid* David to kill me. I don't know who. I'm pretty sure he doesn't even know himself. But whoever it is is out there somewhere. And—" She swiped viciously at her eyes. There was nothing worse than crying in front of people. "And how am I even going to know when they'll try again? Or who they'll pay next time?"

Rae glanced over her shoulder, suddenly completely creeped out. Even now, while she was sitting in the park with Anthony, someone could be watching her, waiting for their chance to strike. She shivered in the warm September sun, realizing just how dangerous her world had become.

turn the page
for a preview of
fingerprints #2:

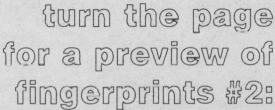

Chapter 1

Rae Voight's clock radio started blaring. Without lifting her head off the pillow, she reached over and jammed the snooze button.

/I'm watching you, Rae/

Rae scrambled out of bed, her heart scraping up against her ribs. Someone had been in her room. A stranger. The thought she'd picked up when she touched the snooze button didn't feel familiar. It wasn't from her dad. It wasn't from Alice, the woman who cleaned their house. It wasn't from anybody who had any reason to be there.

Okay, okay, she told herself. *First thing you need is information.*

"Come on, you freak, tell me who you are," she muttered. She ran her fingers lightly over the radio,

1

then over her nightstand, including the little lamp. *I'm watching you, Rae/***I'm watching you, Rae/***I'm watching you, Rae/***I'm watching you, Rae/***I'm watching you, Rae/*

The thoughts were full of hatred—hatred and fury. She could feel the emotions rush through her body, starting the acid pumping in her stomach, making her knees shake, increasing the temperature of her blood.

No. This can't be happening, Rae thought, her heart now ramming into her ribs. A whole . . . a whole *team* of people couldn't have been in here. It was impossible.

Impossible? Like someone planting a pipe bomb in a bathroom to kill you? Rae asked herself. *'Cause that kind of impossible, it's possible, and you know it*. It hadn't even been that long since it had happened.

Slowly Rae backed way from the nightstand, her eyes locked on it as if it was going to hurl itself off the floor and attack her. She stumbled into her desk chair and grabbed its soft leather back to steady herself.

*/I'm watching you, Rae/I'm watching you, Rae/***I'm watching you, Rae/*

She shoved the chair away from her—

*/***I'm watching you, Rae/***I'm watching you, Rae/*

—and bolted to the door, then wrenched it open.

*/I'm watching you, Rae/***I'm watching you, Rae/*

The hallway was quiet except for the faint sound of Rae's father snoring. She stood perfectly still, trying not to even hear her own breathing. The intruder—no, the *intruders* were gone.

Shower, Rae thought, letting out her breath. Then she could think—really think—about what she should do.

Rae hurried to the bathroom and shoved open the door with her shoulder. She pulled the door closed with two fingers and locked it.

/I'm watching you, Rae/*Watching you*/

Shaking, she switched on the water. These people . . . they had been here, too. Everywhere. What *hadn't* they touched in her home? She stood under the warm spray, the scent of her citrus shower gel filling her nose. She turned away from the nozzle, then leaned back her head and let the water soak her long, curly hair. She'd wash it. Then she'd come up with some kind of—

Rae's eyes locked on the showerhead. There was something glittering behind the dozens of little holes. Every nerve in her body went on red alert. Had they done something to the shower? Was this the second attempt to kill her?

Rae jerked off the water, then pried at the showerhead with her fingernails. She had to get it off, had to see what was under there. One of her nails pulled away from the skin. The pain brought tears to Rae's eyes, but she kept jerking at the showerhead. Finally the part with the little holes came free from the base, and underneath—

"A camera," Rae whispered. She leaned out of the shower and grabbed her toothbrush from the sink.

/Watching you/

3

Ignoring the thoughts from the brush, Rae used it to stab at the tiny camera lense until it cracked, then she scrambled out of the tub, banging her anklebone on the side and managing to step on one of the pieces of glass.

Damn. Rae grabbed one of the big bath sheets off the towel rack and wrapped it around herself. She needed to do a full-house search for more cameras. But she couldn't walk around leaving a blood trail. She balanced on one foot and pulled the piece of glass free, then opened the medicine cabinet—

/I'm watching you, Rae/

—and screamed. A man was peering at her between the little shelves. He reached through and grabbed her by the shoulders. Shook her.

"Rae," the man exclaimed. He sounded like her father.

Rae's eyes flew open, and she saw her father standing over her, his blue eyes locked on her face. She sat up, pulling free of his grasp.

Oh God, it was a dream, she realized, glancing down at the blanket clutched in her hand.

"Sorry. I guess that dream scream came out real, huh?" she asked, trying to sound normal.

"I'll say," her father answered. "It must have been quite a nightmare." He waited, and Rae knew he was expecting her to tell him what it was about. But she didn't want to think about it for even a few seconds more.

4

"Yeah," she answered. She glanced at her clock radio. 4:01. "But I have time to get in a good dream before I have to get up." She hoped she didn't sound as freaked as she felt. She didn't want her dad to start worrying. For months that's all he'd done—worry about her.

"Let me get you a glass of water," he said.

"That's okay," Rae answered, but he was already out the door. Rae used both hands to shove her hair away from her face. The roots were damp with sweat.

It was just a dream, she told herself. But that didn't make her feel any better. Yeah, it was just a dream. But it was a dream that was all about what she was afraid of in real life. Someone out there wanted her dead. And she had no idea who. Or when they might try again.

Rae's dad hurried back in with the water and pressed the glass into her hand.

/thought she was getting better/

"It was just a dream, Dad," she said, wanting him to believe it, even though it wasn't really true. Wanting him to believe that their lives were back to normal, that even though she'd spent the summer in a mental hospital, she was fine, fine, fine. "Just a dream," she repeated, then pulled the covers up as high as she could. But she still felt chilled, as if her spine had turned to ice.

Rae headed toward the cafeteria, trying to exude . . . just your basic normalcy. For years there'd been nothing she wanted more than getting noticed. And she'd done it. She'd been right there in the center, girlfriend of Marcus Salkow, Sanderson's It boy. Then she'd had her little freak-out—make that humongous freak-out—in the caf the day she first started getting the not-her thoughts and been sent off to the walnut farm, and now her biggest ambition was to blend.

Which wasn't all that easy. People were still way too interested in whether or not she was going to have another meltdown to take their eyes off her for long. Rae's steps slowed down. Or did one of them have a different reason for staring? Could one of the people checking her out be the person who wanted her dead? Her eyes jumped from face to face. It seemed ridiculous to think that anyone who went to her school had tried to kill her. They spent all their time planning what to wear and how to get invited to the best parties, and, if they were ambitious, how to get the SAT scores to make it into the college Mom and Dad had their hearts set on. But that was it. Right?

Rae did another quick face scan. When her eyes fell on Jeff Brunner, he blushed the color of an overripe tomato, then lowered his head so he wouldn't have to look at her.

All he needs is a sign that says Kick Me, I'm Scum, Rae thought.

But Jeff wasn't acting all guilty because he'd tried to

off her. No, all scum boy had done was decide Rae was such a loser that she'd be *grateful* to let him into her pants. Fortunately Rae'd gotten that piece of info from his fingerprints before Jeff had even gotten close to scoring, and she'd put the little weasel in his place. She watched him scurry into the guys' bathroom like the rodent he was.

It's gonna be a while before he decides to try his luck with another "loser" girl, Rae thought with satisfaction.

She continued down the hallway, almost bumping into a guy who stepped away from the drinking fountain without bothering to look where he was going. "Sorry," he said, turning to face her.

Marcus Salkow. Rae's heart gave a jerk and ended up somewhere in her throat. *The parade of the scum boys continues,* she thought, trying to get a grip.

"Um, how's it going, Rae?" he asked, looking somewhere near her face but not directly at it.

"Fine," she mumbled, heart still slamming around in her throat like a bird that wanted to get out. God, while Marcus couldn't look at her, she couldn't *stop* staring at him. Did he have to be so gorgeous? He was like a poster boy for prep school. A clean-cut, football-player-muscled, blond, green-eyed example of a young southern gentleman. "Fine," Rae muttered again. She continued down the hall, not wanting to drag out the encounter, afraid if she looked at him another second, she'd start drooling or something equally humiliating.

7

You let him off so easy, she thought. Rae hadn't allowed Jeff to treat her like dirt. Why should Marcus be any different?

Because I loved him, Rae answered herself. *Because I thought he loved me.* Which actually made what Marcus did to her a million times worse.

Without giving herself time to reconsider, Rae spun around and hurried back up to him, ignoring the way her heart now seemed to fill every inch of her body. Pounding, pounding, pounding. "When I said I'm fine, it was true," Rae told him, her words coming out clipped and hard. "Except for the fact that I came back to school and found out that you're with Dori Hernandez, which no one bothered to tell me." She hauled in a deep, shuddering breath. "Including you."

Marcus didn't answer. He just continued to do that not-quite-looking-at-her thing. Rae took a quarter step to the side, putting herself directly into his line of vision. Her heart-body pounded harder.

"Look. I'm sorry," Marcus finally said. "You were in the hospital, and I didn't think it was a good idea to upset you by telling you . . . you know. I was worried about you." Marcus gave a helpless shrug, then reached out and pushed a lock of her curly hair away from her face. "Really worried," he added softly.

Rae shrank back from his hand. She didn't want him touching her, especially because it still did something to her, started turning her all soft inside. "You were so worried, you never came to visit."

"I came—" he began to protest.

"Once," she interrupted. "People I've barely said hi to came once."

He clicked his teeth together nervously. She'd seen him do the same thing in class when he got called on and didn't know the answer. Rae's heart returned to its usual place in her chest, and the pounding eased up, leaving her feeling numb and hollowed out.

"Rae, it's just that . . ." Marcus's words trailed off.

Before he could start clicking again, Rae jumped in. "Whatever, Marcus. Go find Dori." She turned and walked away. When she reached the cafeteria's double doors, she used her shoulder to open the closest one and slipped inside. She didn't want to hear anyone else's thoughts right now. Her own were more than enough.

She felt a tap on her shoulder and nearly jumped, then spun around.

"Yogurt?" Lea Dessin asked.

Rae's shoulders relaxed. It wasn't her would-be killer—just the best friend who'd totally abandoned her.

"Yogurt," Rae agreed. She didn't have the energy to do anything else.

Lea led the way over to the fro-yo machines, her sleek black hair shining under the fluorescent lights. This felt so normal. But it wasn't. Not anymore.

Because now Lea was afraid of Rae. She never said it, of course. And she didn't even really act like it. But Rae knew it was true. Fingerprints didn't lie.

"Do you want to sit?" Lea jerked her chin toward the usual table—correction, what used to be the usual table—as she made her fro-yo sculpture.

She's trying, Rae thought. *Even though she's scared of me, she's trying.*

"Could we maybe be adventurous and—"

"Sit someplace else?" Lea finished for her, still sounding just a little too peppy. *Clearly overcompensating,* Rae decided as Lea moved out of the way so Rae could get to the frozen yogurt machine.

"Just for today," Rae answered, grabbing a cup and a spoon—new, no prints. She didn't want Lea to think she was going to have to spend all year baby-sitting her freaky used-to-be best friend. But for this one day it would be so nice just to sit with someone and look normal, a normal girl with a normal friend. No psi power. No streak of insanity. No one out to kill her.

Rae took a napkin out of the metal holder and used it to pull down the handle. "It's always sticky," she explained to Lea as the yogurt spiraled into the cup. God, she wouldn't want to see Lea's expression if she heard the truth.

See, if I touch the handle after you touched it, I'll know your thoughts. And really, I'd rather not.

Because you deserve some privacy. And I deserve not to hear how creepy you think I am.

Lea was scared enough already. Hearing the truth would probably send *her* to the funny farm. Ha ha. Hee hee.

"There's a place over there." Lea nodded at a couple of empty seats that were about halfway across the room from the usual table.

"Looks good," Rae answered, leading the way. She took a seat, and Lea sat down across from her. *Now what?* Rae thought. *What am I supposed to say?* Something nonfrightening. Something normal. But what?

"So, do you already have a ton of homework? I'm buried," Rae said. Pathetic. But at least it was words.

"Yeah, me too." Lea shot a glance over Rae's shoulder. *What is she looking at?* Rae wondered. Then she got it. Lea was looking at *the* table, watching Jackie and Vince and Marcus and *Dori.*

Rae got an image in her head of a massive steel door swinging shut, separating her old life—her prehospital, prefingerprint power life—from her new life. Lea was on one side. Lea and Marcus and Vince and Jackie and all Rae's old friends. And Rae was on the other. All alone.

Don't get all soap opera, she told herself. *You're not alone. Dad's on your side of the door. And . . . and Anthony Fascinelli and Jesse Beven.* Both the guys from group therapy knew the truth about her psychic ability. Anthony was the one who'd helped her figure out where all the strange thoughts were coming from. And he and Jesse were both okay with it.

And don't forget Yana, Rae reminded herself. Yana Savari had been a volunteer at the hospital. When she'd asked Rae to exchange numbers, Rae'd thought Yana was just taking her on as a charity case. But Yana was turning into a real friend. A Lea kind of friend, before Lea got all weirded out by Rae.

So get over yourself, Rae thought. She had friends. Maybe not a lot of them—but enough.

"Um, I'm taking chemistry this year, and forget about it. Just the work from that class is killer," Lea said. She took a bite of her yogurt.

Rae took a spoonful of her own. When Lea snuck another glance at her usual table, Rae pretended not to notice. What was the point of making a big deal about it? She and Lea wouldn't be doing this again.

Where the hell is she? Anthony Fascinelli checked his watch. It was still ten minutes before their group therapy session started up. But Rae should be here.

What if whoever had hired David Wyngard to set that pipe bomb and off Rae had already tried again? Or hired someone else to do it? What if she was lying dead somewhere? His stomach did a slow roll. What if—

And then he saw her. Walking across the parking lot like one of those girls in a shampoo commercial, her curly reddish brown hair all bouncy, looking like she owned the world and everyone should just fall at her feet if she smiled at them.

She wasn't being careful. She couldn't look like that—all shampoo commercial girl—and be observing everything that was going on around her. What was wrong with her?

"You're late," Anthony snapped as she approached him. "And you're stupid."

She glanced at her slim silver watch. "I'm early," she corrected him. She didn't bother responding to the stupid part.

"What's been going on the last few days? Have you noticed anything unusual? Have you noticed *anything?*" He wanted to reach out, grab her by the shoulders, and shake her. Instead he jammed his hands in the pockets of his jeans. "Has there been a strange car in your neighborhood? Someone you don't really know trying to get all friendly at school? Someone—"

"A stranger in a van offering me candy if I get inside?" Rae interrupted.

"Is that supposed to be funny?" Anthony demanded. He took a step closer and lowered his voice. "Someone is trying to kill you, remember? I can't believe you're acting like it's all a big joke."

"What do you want me to do? I have no idea who hired David to kill me. Not a clue. Am I supposed to walk around being afraid of everybody? Is that what you want?"

Her voice had this tremor running through it, and Anthony realized she wasn't all shampoo girl casual. Pretty much the opposite. "I just want you to be safe," he muttered.

"Yeah, well, I want that, too. But it's not like I can be suspicious of the whole world. I'd end up back in the nuthouse," Rae answered.

"We'll figure something out," Anthony said. Although he had no idea how. He shifted from foot to foot, not knowing what to say next. "I guess we should go in," he finally added.

"We're not waiting for Jesse?" Rae asked.

"If we do, we'll all be late, and Abramson will be three times as pissed," Anthony said. He led the way inside and down to the group therapy room. Most of the metal chairs were already filled, but there were two together by the door. He sat down in one, and Rae slipped into the one next to him. He'd feel a lot better if he could keep her this close all the time. Not that he'd be able to do any good if someone came at her with a gun or something.

Ms. Abramson hurried into the room, pulling Anthony away from his thoughts. She shut the door behind her and strode to the center of the circle. She was wearing one of those sleeveless dresses again. Anthony figured she had to lift weights because her dark arms were all muscle, none of that jelly at the tops like a lot of women her age had.

"I have a couple of announcements before we start," Abramson said. She flipped one of her many braids back over her shoulder. "First, Anthony Fascinelli was not responsible for the pipe bomb. I'm sure you all heard that Mr. Rocha found materials for a bomb in Anthony's backpack, but they were put there by David Wyngard. Obviously David will no longer be a member of our group." She turned her gaze to Anthony, her eyes bright with emotion. "On behalf of Mr. Rocha and myself, I want to apologize for making a judgment too quickly and to welcome Anthony back."

Yeah, right, Anthony thought. He could believe Abramson felt bad and wanted him back in group. But there was no way the director of the institute was all happy Anthony was back at Oakvale. Rocha'd been totally psyched to have a reason to give Anthony the boot.

Abramson began to pace back and forth across the center of the circle. "My other announcement is a disturbing one. I got a call from Jesse Beven's mother."

Anthony sat up straight, the bones of his spine suddenly feeling sharp against his flesh.

"Mrs. Beven told me that Jesse has run away," Abramson continued. "I'm sure this news will bring up all kinds of feelings, and I wanted to take the first part of our session to talk about them."

No way. No freakin' way.

He leaned toward Rae, the bones of his back biting into his muscles. "This is crap," he whispered. "Jesse wouldn't bolt. Not without saying something to me."

"So what do you think happened?" Rae whispered back.

"I don't know. But I'm going to find out," Anthony promised.